CONFEDERATE STATES

a novel

By

T.R. Pearson

BARKING MAD PRESS

2020

SUGAR BIT

i

I only followed him because he ran right past me in his underpants, some big hairy guy carrying a hot pink lunchbox. By the time I got the car turned around, he was a quarter-mile up the road where he tossed that lunchbox into a bush and veered off the pavement and vanished.

I radioed in, and Lori was reminded of a man she'd once seen tubing on the Rappahannock. He'd not been wearing a thing in the world but socks.

"Take your spray," she told me.

Of course, spray was all I had. We don't get guns or even sticks but just a Ford Fiesta, a blue uniform, a plastic whistle, and a can of pepper gel.

I located a gap in the thicket big enough for a man to pass through, but there was nobody on the other side, just a slew of half-built houses. I came back to find that pink lunchbox snagged high in an autumn olive and went to hunt a limb to knock it loose.

There was what looked like a bunch of junk inside. A few Polaroid pictures stuck together. A doll about the size of a Barbie with one arm gone and no head. A mint tin with four brass buttons in it. The husk of a cicada. A little sandwich bag that held a couple of filthy stones. Three clothespins with rusty hinges, a matchbook from some place called Mo's, and a tiny tarnished Jesus on a tiny tarnished cross.

I well knew I should drop that lunchbox off with Lori at the end of my shift, but she'd just shove it in the cupboard where all the stray stuff went and hold it there against the day the owner came to claim it. She wouldn't care he couldn't know to and so surely never would.

Instead, I decided to say nothing to her and carry it home to Russell since the job I'm working is kind of his anyway. He'd been auxiliary police for a year and a bit when he had his stroke. Now he stays at the house while I stand in for him until he's fit and recovered. They didn't have to let me, but Lori and them settled on the decent thing.

I drive Russell's old Fiesta with his yellow light on the roof, the magnetic kind that needs a cord to trail down through the window. The inside still smells of him a little – his aftershave, his smokes – and the glovebox is crammed with his receipts and junk. I thought he'd be in better shape after seven months, but Russell still lurches when he walks and can't move one arm at all. He makes noises that aren't remotely words. He eats baby food. He drools.

No woman marries a man expecting anything like this, though I can't say Russell was ever much of a catch. I was on the rebound when I met him, looking to spite my former intended who'd thrown me over for a divorcee he'd snagged at a church retreat. So I was motivated to ignore Russell's various deficiencies. His paunch, his bald spot, his third-hand Buick, his tenth-grade education.

I was a cashier at the Dollar Tree when a man came in to rob it. He accused me of being lippy and smacked me hard once with his gun. That's why Russell took the job with Lori in the first place. He had hopes of finding Dollar Tree boy and visiting vengeance on him, but nobody ever saw the guy again.

We drive the streets where cars were stolen or property vandalized and make a show of being vigilant and something bordering on official. We loop through lots at office parks and patrol industrial sites, swing by churches and public schools in evenings and off-hours. If you come across actual lawlessness, you raise Lori on the squawker. Sometimes she'll even call a proper cop.

They don't always show because, as a rule, they think we're

dopes and meddlers, and a few of our crew have charged into trouble with just their whistles and spray. Not me. I've got a dodgy hip, thirty extra pounds of bloat, and I'm usually a fair few minutes trying to get out of the car.

Ordinarily, then, I don't come home with workaday stories worth telling, so the underpants guy made for an exotic treat. Once we'd finished supper and I'd gotten Russell swabbed down and tidied up, I set that lunchbox on the kitchen table.

"Had me kind of a day," is what I said.

Russell knew the location well. A clump of abandoned warehouses with the suburbs crowding in.

"Big fellow," I told him. "Slipped up on me. Wasn't wearing a thing but briefs."

Russell mounted one of his involved runs of sinusy palaver. I nodded like I knew what he was going on about, but it had gotten to where everything Russell said was only noise to me.

I emptied that lunchbox out on the table so Russell could sort through all the junk. Before his stroke, he'd been on something of an investigating jag and had come to believe he had an aptitude for working mysteries out.

It started with a pocketbook Russell found in a ditch. The thing was empty but for a dry cleaning stub he carried around to laundries, and he managed to track down the owner, even drove out to her house. Her handbag was kind of torn up. It looked to have been run over, so she was a little short of delighted to get it back.

I sat by while Russell eyed the things I'd spilled onto the table, and he seemed happy enough to shove them around for the balance of the evening.

That might have been as far as it went if I'd not rolled up on those people. I was on my usual route patrolling all my usual places when I spied a gray sedan parked out by the same warehouses. It was a Chevy with a Florida tag that read U-DALE17.

At first, I couldn't put anybody with it but caught sight of them after a bit. They were well down the way where the guy in his briefs had veered off through the thicket. A man and a woman, as best I could tell, both wearing business suits.

Once they saw me, they both came right on up. I sat and waited with my window cracked and took occasion to radio Lori. I described the car and read out the tag. She was reminded of an old boyfriend of hers, some Dale from out in the valley. I was hearing about the birthmark Lori's Dale had on his privates by the time that pair from the thicket finally arrived.

"Want to come out here?"

The lady was doing the talking. She was lean and rangy, looked nearly six feet tall, and had a haircut she might have given herself with a steak knife in the dark.

"Who y'all with?" I asked back. I didn't move to open my door.

"You around here regular?" she wanted to know.

I went with a shrug like I couldn't quite say.

"We're looking for a man. Might have come through here. Big guy. Dent in his head." She showed me where. "He might have seemed like…disturbed."

"Why don't you come on out here." Now her partner was talking to me. He was thick and short and sweaty and had a scab across his nose. One on his forehead too like maybe he'd hit a tree trunk at a trot.

I stayed where I was. "Florida?" That struck me as something worth asking. "What brings y'all way up here?"

The woman rested an arm on the roof of my car.

"Sugar bit," is how she started.

I hate that sort of thing. It's hard enough being old and dumpy without people calling you doll and dearie and stuff.

"Don't you worry yourself with this." She smacked my roof a couple of times, and then they headed off to their Chevy and pulled out with quite a lot of zip.

I raised Lori again and told her about it. She'd been rooting around and had located her old boyfriend's Facebook page.

"He hasn't held up," she told me.

I didn't bother to say, "What does?"

The rest of my shift was dead ordinary. I showed up at all my places, rolled through slowly to be seen, and then swung by those warehouses one more time in case that pair had come back. I wouldn't have driven clear from Florida to get run off by the likes of me.

But the place was deserted except for a Mexican on the far side of the thicket. He was digging some kind of trench next to one of those half-built houses. We eyed each other but couldn't even be bothered to nod.

Back at home, I found Russell wedged between the toilet and the wall. He'd end up there routinely when he'd refuse to wear his diaper and would attempt to handle his business on his own. He didn't have the skill for it anymore, so I worked him loose like always. As I sluiced him down on his shower chair, I told him who I'd seen.

He said a string of stuff I couldn't understand. I said back "Yeah" and "All right" like I do.

I don't personally have any use for mysteries, not the sort on television where rascals scheme and slink around but get caught anyway or the real-life kind where regular people do a felonious thing and then run loose until some buddy has a drink.

We got that lunchbox out again, but the stuff inside still came across as random junk to me. If I have a personal aptitude, it's for vinegary commentary, so the boy who smacked me in the Dollar Tree wasn't entirely out of line.

Russell said a bunch of something after a while and grabbed the keys from the catchall bowl. Some things I couldn't help but understand.

He looked shabby enough at home, but he looked awful out in public, even if "public" was just some warehouses waiting to get knocked down. Russell's sweatshirt was stained with food and mess. His sweatpants were stained with worse, and he was wearing a pair of sneakers I'd had to pull the laces from to make room for Russell's swollen, crusty feet. I hadn't shaved him in three or four weeks, so he had neck fur and fluffy patches, and his combover had gone feral and was just flopping wherever it pleased.

Once I'd helped him out of the car, Russell waved me off with his good arm to make it plain that he'd be sniffing around alone. I watched him from up alongside the Ford in case he toppled over. By that time, I wasn't so terribly curious about the Florida people and was ready to write off underwear guy as one of life's random things. I figured he had pressure building up and had just come a little undone.

My mother was kind of like that. She used to climb into the corn crib and sing "Teach Me O Lord Thy Holy Way" whenever her stuff got out of hand.

Russell had plunged deep into the shrubbery by the time I heard him squawking, so I headed down, and he showed me a bunch of mess he'd come across – a Mars Bar wrapper, a Bud Lite can, a busted butane lighter, a greasy burger sack, a caulking tube, a flattened cigarette pack. He had me help him pick it up and carry it all home.

Russell wanted our den for his incident room, but I wouldn't let him have it. Instead, I gave him the puny back bedroom we'd never put furniture in. There were sacks of my skinny clothes in there and three or four boxes of Russell's sister's junk, grubby stuff she'd bought at flea markets and yard sales. If that woman could get a thing cut-rate, she didn't much care what it was.

Russell gathered up a roll of tape, a spool of string, and a couple of felt-tipped markers and then retired to the back bedroom to try to work this mystery out.

By that time, I should confess, I was borderline finished with Russell. I'd been screwing up the nerve to leave him right before he had his stroke, and there I was stuck nearly eight months later with Russell not really improving and me having to wipe him and wash him and feed him and work his job.

As far as I know, Russell stayed all night messing around in the back bedroom, and the next day after work I swung by the superstore to pick up fluids for our Ford. Whatever that Fiesta didn't incinerate, it was all but certain to leak, and I was making my way to automotive when I glanced down a grocery aisle and saw a man who looked familiar to me. At first, I couldn't say just why.

He was reading the back of a soup can, and I kept wondering how I knew him. I'd gotten as far as the fishing tackle when I told myself, "Hold on."

He'd moved on to a noodle box by the time I found him again.

"Hey," I said.

He glanced my way.

"You're the guy in his underpants, right?"

The longer I looked at him, the less sure of that I was, so about all he would have had to do was shake his head to put me off. Instead, he set his noodles down and lit out in a hurry. I followed him towards the front of the store and quizzed him as we went.

"Is you, isn't it?"

He kept going.

"I saw you out there. Remember?"

He didn't slow down at all.

"Found that lunchbox of yours," I told him.

That served to stop him quick. He passed a quarter minute in study of the floor.

"Funny stuff in there."

He turned my way. The man looked dangerous all of a sudden, so I headed down a cosmetics aisle and through to the greeting cards where I found a woman blowing up balloons. I told her all about the customer who was making me uneasy, and she walkie-talkied to scare up their off-duty cop.

He escorted me clear out to my car and sneered at my uniform on the way. He complained about some colleague of mine I didn't know named Norman who'd recently made a colossal hash of a burglary arrest.

"Got all in the damn way," that cop told me, and once we'd reached my Ford, he said, "You people," instead of maybe "Good luck and goodbye."

I felt sure underwear guy was lying for me somewhere in the lot. I'd decided he was just the sort to follow a woman home so he could knock her around and strangle her with a lamp cord. Consequently, I took an especially peculiar route back to our house and made all kinds of detours and crazy turns. I left the Fiesta at the AME church up the road and crossed backyards to get home.

Once I'd slipped in through our carshed door, I barged straight into the back bedroom.

"I saw him," I told Russell, and I was about to explain just who when the state of the place pretty much struck me dumb.

I'd heard Russell bumping around in there, but I hadn't so much as peeked in. He'd taped lunchbox items and thicket trash all across the back wall and had run string between whatever he'd decided was connected. That appeared to be nearly everything since there was string all over the place.

I squinted at some of the marker scrawl Russell had Sharpied straight onto the wall, but his writing hand only half worked, so it looked part Klingon and part Chinese.

"Saw underwear guy in the Walmart," I told him, "and there's a better than decent chance he followed me home."

I advised Russell to get our gun and take it onto the porch. We had a pistol Russell's sister had bought at some tag sale for next to nothing. It was rusty and in three pieces and seemed to be missing the firing pin, but it could pass for lethal if you held it right and didn't actually need to shoot it. Russell grabbed the thing out of one of her boxes and went lurching up the hall.

I had no time much to linger and study his work because he yelled for me right away. I hustled out to the driveway to find him pointing that rickety pistol at our neighbor from across the road, the one who was always making a fuss about racket on the block. He got migraine headaches and took medicine for them, which he fairly lived to bring up.

His name was Clarence, but he was always desperate for people to call him C-Bog. It chafed him that nobody ever would. He had a motorcycle he never rode and a pet tree squirrel named Leon. He worked as a counselor advising hooligans once they were doing county time.

As soon as Clarence had stepped my way a little, I could see somebody beyond him. That's who Russell had actually set up the fuss about.

Clarence complained to me about Russell hollering in the driveway, told me he was taking Eletriptan for his head. Then he spelled it out the way he almost always did.

Russell yelled something else, and Clarence announced he found the racket provoking. He was upset enough to close on Russell and give him a half-hearted shove. For some reason, underwear guy objected and pitched Clarence into the street from where Clarence spelled Eletriptan another time and told us about a cop he knew.

Once he'd finished, I said to underwear guy, "Russell'll shoot you if that's what you need."

The man snorted at me like a stallion might.

"Is this about your lunchbox?" There seemed no point in dodging around, especially since he'd done us the favor of putting Clarence on the ground.

That was enough to earn me a grunt and nod.

"All right. Fine," I told him. "We don't even want it." With that, I waved the man into the house where I led him down the hall to the back spare room.

Russell came lurching along and started explaining exactly what he'd been up to. That's what I decided he was doing anyway. He took underwear guy by the arm and walked him to the far wall where they had what resembled, for all the world, a genuine conversation.

It was like watching a foreign movie nobody had bothered to dub. When Russell talked, I couldn't begin to tell what he was saying, and when underwear guy raised a racket, I could only guess what he meant.

Then the doorbell rang. It turned out to be Clarence and his friend the cop. I'd seen him before. He was squat and dumpy and looked like he shaved about once a week.

"Where is he?" the cop friend asked me. No preamble, no introductions, which is standard cop stuff for our end of town. Then we all heard those two in the spare room doing their sort of talking, so he pushed on past me and headed down the hall.

The cop was prepared to let Clarence be gracious. That wasn't, however, Clarence's usual way, so underwear guy ended up in handcuffs with his pockets emptied onto the floor. A half pack of gum. A stubby pencil like you'd use at Putt-Putt and a couple of car keys on a ring. He told that cop his name was Doug, but he didn't have ID.

"What do you want to do?" I asked Russell once Doug had been hauled off.

He said a lot of something back and then went out to the car.

We had a new police station west of town on the far side of everything. It was even beyond the used-car lots and the pay-as-you-go medical clinic. That cop shop looked like a branch bank gone thyroidal.

We sat around for half an hour in a waiting room that would have suited a muffler shop. There was a TV tuned to one of those shows where a couple buys a fixer-upper and then realizes what they truly need is a divorce.

I was still wearing my uniform, which proved to be kind of a problem since I got to hear from the guy at the desk and a couple of cops in passing about trouble they'd had with colleagues of mine who'd stuck their noses all up in stuff.

"I don't ever get out of the car," I finally told a sergeant.

He sized me up with a look and a laugh. "Guess not," is what he said.

There was a nervous lady in there with us. She was waiting for somebody she only ever called "baby." She kept telling us, "Baby ain't the one they want."

She appeared to be medicated, had dosed herself with whatever might make you sweat and twitch and chew skin off your thumbs.

At first, hearing Russell talk appeared to rattle her but good. Eventually, she worked up the nerve to ask me, "Something wrong with him?"

She seemed delighted when I told her, "Yes."

She opened up after that and proved to be one of those people who'd decided what she thought about nearly everything, especially the stuff she knew next to nothing about. I'd had all of her I could stand by the time Clarence's cop came out.

He walked us back to a room where Clarence and Doug were parked at a table. Clarence was polishing off a pack of nabs. Doug was shackled to an eyebolt.

"Won't give us nothing but a first name," the cop said.

"Can't help you," I told him. "Only known him for an hour."

"Here's what we're thinking. He apologizes, and we let it go at that."

"Could have done that back home." I was talking to Clarence by then.

"I was still hot," Clarence allowed. "Head was kind of throbbing." He'd spelled about half of Eletriptan before his cop friend cut him off.

"Good good?" that fellow wanted to know.

Clarence nodded. Doug nodded some too.

Because Clarence had ridden over in the radio car, he hitched a ride with us back home, which made for a cozy trip in our Fiesta.

"Didn't have to be this way," he said about every quarter mile.

I don't know what he was hoping to hear. Doug and Russell weren't doing much talking, and I was having to drive with my seat so far up I could barely breathe.

"Could have gone different." That was Clarence working a variation. "You ain't got to knock people over."

I was about to tell him it would have gone different if nobody had called the damn police, but then Doug stepped on my seatbelt, and I think I blacked out for a bit.

It was probably near midnight by the time we got home, and I had to be up and on the job at eight, so I was more than ready for Doug to take off for wherever it was he stayed, but Russell had different ideas, and those two went straight into the spare room. I didn't wait around for them to come out but turned in for the night. When I woke up at half-past six in the morning, I was alone in the house.

ii

I'm not the worrying sort, and it wasn't like Russell hadn't taken off before. He'd go on walkabouts whenever he got exasperated. I found him all the way out at the farm supply once after a visit with his doctor, and another time he went clear to the old Richmond road for reasons I never made out. Usually, somebody would call me to fetch him, though sometimes he'd just find his way home.

So I wasn't fretting. I had my bowl of oatmeal and my coffee and then took a leisurely tour of the spare room by way of sniffing around. Somebody with passable penmanship – I figured it must have been Doug – had written Del-Jo-Ray on the wall alongside some of Russell's scrawl. I knew it for the name of a trailer park out by a string of mill ponds. The place had been scenic until a dam failed and the water leaked away.

I'd been out there once to pick up a table lamp I'd bought from a woman online. When I showed up, she tried to give me a different, trashier lamp, and we quarreled. She asked me in a shirty way if I was calling her a liar, and I told her with my usual dose of vinegar I was.

A sign was planted out front of Del-Jo-Ray Acres that a woodworker had made. It even looked to have been a classy item before the weather got to it along with a few salty humans who'd sprung for some Rustoleum.

I ran immediately across a boy on a bike who might have been twelve or twenty-three with rickets. He was shirtless and scrawny and had enough grit in his ears for a going crop.

I described Doug and Russell and asked if he'd seen them.

"You the law?"

"No."

"Ain't nobody around here can't talk." He said it with what I'll call a hint of rue. Then he spat on the ground in a showy way and rode off doing a wheelie.

I next tried a grown man in pajama bottoms and a large woman in just stretchy pants and a bra. They were both beyond unhelpful, more like anti-helpful. The man had seen a guy like Doug once out in Cincinnati while the woman said her neighbor two lots over ate saltines and molasses every damn day for dessert.

I ended up going back to the lady with the lamp, knocked on her door anyway, but a different woman answered. This one was learning to give psychic readings with the help of playing cards, not because she had some special insight into human nature or tools to use beyond what proved a ratty pinochle deck, but mostly because she was chasing an employment opportunity from a gentleman up the road with a tattoo parlor and a stall to rent out cheap.

"You have trouble in your life," she told me before I'd gotten well inside. She did her stuff on a coffee table she hadn't quite bothered to clear.

"I'm looking for a man," I volunteered.

She said back, of course, "I know."

She had me call her Lady Angela and then wondered how I liked it. Her given name was Cheryl, but that didn't strike her as psychic enough.

"Did he give you that ring, your man?"

"No."

"Figured." Lady Angela laid out four cards face up.

"It belonged to my mother," I told her.

She said she'd known that too even if, in fact, I'd pinched it from a cousin.

"Your mother was beautiful," Lady Angela said while considering a ten of diamonds. "But she had trouble in her life." That struck me as a safe strategy for a psychic reader who'd be working out of a stall in a tattoo shop.

"Looking for two men really. One of them's big, like six and a half feet tall."

That got Lady Angela off her cards for a moment. "Hairy?"

"That's him. Got kind of a dent in his head."

"They stayed around the corner for a couple of days. The one that's painted blue."

"They?"

"Girl too. Little thing." Lady Angela lit a cigarette. "Dressed like some kind of baby doll."

I gave her five dollars. That was also the price I'd paid for the wrong lamp.

The blue trailer was easy enough to find, and the door to it was standing wide open.

I beat on the siding. "Anybody home?"

A duck came out and joined me on what passed for the front porch, which was just a slew of cinder blocks nobody had leveled up. He was a regular duck, white and orange, the kind you'd throw bread at in a park. He gurgled at me in a ducky way and then pecked the top of my shoe.

Aside from having no interest in mysteries, I'm not a nervy woman either, so I was pleased when that duck elected to turn around and lead me inside.

The thing was a standard-issue single wide. A sofa and a recliner. A table that looked like it would fold into the wall. A bathroom a man the size of Doug could maybe turn around in, and a bedroom that was barely big enough to fit the bed. There were no personal items I could see beyond a cup in one of the cupboards with *Be-atch!* printed on it. The duck, for his part, just gurgled and crapped occasionally on the floor.

Back outside I stopped for a moment in what passed for the front yard. It was dirt and weeds and weathered trash along with a painted rock border. The duck was loitering there alongside me when the gas man rolled in and dragged his hose to a tank just up the road.

He thought I was a Jehovah's Witness or something there at

first and so told me like you'd tell a dog, "Go on," but then I pointed out my uniform, which finally did me some good.

"Was he one of yours?" I asked and had a glance at Doug's blue trailer.

He nodded.

"Know him much?"

He shook his head.

"This his duck?"

"Lady," he said, "I just bring the gas."

That duck hopped into my Fiesta before I could get away. He jumped straight through the window and hunkered down on the passenger seat like a bird who'd done some riding around before. Since I didn't mind the company, I just left him alone.

I swung by our place, but Russell still wasn't at home, so I drove over to those derelict warehouses on the chance Doug and Russell had gone there to snoop around. I left the Fiesta parked up top and went for a walk along the thicket. The duck stayed back at the car until he changed his mind and came sailing by on the wing. He landed with all the grace of a head of cabbage, the way ducks will.

I decided on the spot I'd call him Rusty, the name of the horse I'd never owned. I suspected he'd answer to that about as well as *hey* and *duck*.

Me and Rusty passed through a gap in the thicket and wandered around that half-built neighborhood where nobody was even close to moving in. Some of those houses looked like they'd been abandoned for a while, and I could hear from the racket that one or two were having work done on them. There was a drill going somewhere, and a boy up the way was running one of those junior diggers.

"Guess the money dried up," I said to Rusty who did a little flying, but mostly he ran along the ground and gurgled and squawked and pecked.

We headed for the nearest house, a colonial with no doors. There was nothing inside but empty drink cans and scattered tubes of adhesive, so we moved on to the next one where we turned up two electricians having a squabble. They couldn't see eye to eye about a woman named Linda who one of them had been married to and the other had picked up in a bar.

He was the one who said, "Seems all right."

Her ex was the one who said, "Isn't."

Then they both explained to me just who they were talking about and why.

"I'm looking for a man," I told them. "Maybe two. Can't really be sure."

"Ain't nobody here," the ex-husband said.

"Yeah, why is that?" I asked them since I had the chance.

"Something with the bank." That from the barfly. "Your duck?"

Rusty wandered and gurgled.

"Looking like it."

"I had a goose once," the ex-husband said. "Won't be doing that again."

"Did y'all happen to be around when the guy came running through half-naked?"

They decided they couldn't agree about that as well.

I kept thinking I'd put Rusty out at the first pond I came across, but he was such good company in the car that I carried him all the way home. Since there was still no sign of Russell, I thought I'd best call the police, and a lady cop came rolling up after a while. I say a lady, but she was more like a block of suet with eye liner and a bun.

I told her about Russell to give her a fair sense of how helpless he was and had started in on Doug a little when Rusty set up a fuss in the bathroom where I'd decided to shut him up. We could hear him squawking and flapping and banging around.

"New duck," I told the woman.

She made a noise in her throat and pulled out a card with the number of a crisis line on it. She assured me there was no shame in making the call.

I kept a cat once for a girl I knew. She had to drive clear to Baton Rouge for some relation's funeral and didn't think her cat would hold up well alone. He made so much mischief loose in my house that I shut him up in the bathroom where he had (I guess) a full-blown cat conniption. He worked the toilet roll off its spindle and kicked it all over the place. He pulled the towels onto the floor and peed on them until they were soaked through. He clawed at all the wallpaper he could reach and even gouged the plaster beneath it. He brought down the shower curtain rod, plugged the toilet with a washcloth, and he still found time to swat at me under the door when I'd stray near.

That cat, though, had nothing on Rusty who knocked over the laundry hamper and doused all the clothes that spilled out with greasy, white diarrhea, which appeared to be the only kind of movement he ever had. He left streaks of it on the walls, even splashed some onto the ceiling. He'd also flipped the throw rug over and pecked off the rubber underneath.

He calmed down as soon as I let him out. Rusty followed me into the kitchen where he flew up onto the stovetop and parked himself in a greasy skillet. I gave him a hamburger roll to work on and poured three fingers of scotch for me. Then I sat at the dinette to weigh my options. I figured I could either wait for Russell to come home on his own or go out and ride the roads across the county.

Of course, I wasn't nearly as frantic as a loving wife would have been, and I poured me a splash more whiskey, gave Rusty another hamburger roll, and then turned back around to find that I had company in the kitchen. I hadn't heard a thing, but I'd been joined by the woman with the hair.

"I knocked," she said.

"Did not."

"Might be closer to it." She squinted past me towards the stovetop. "That's no way to cook a duck."

"Did you find them or something?" I asked her.

"Who?"

"Russell and Doug."

"Don't know a Russell. Don't believe I know a Doug."

"How'd you even find me?"

"They picked up a man here last night, right?"

"Doug," I said and nodded.

"Kelvin," she told me. "We're kind of looking for him. More his girlfriend really. Where's your crapper?"

I gave her directions but failed to warn her, so she shouted back, "Sweet Christ!"

I didn't catch her name. Never caught it and only ever called her U-Dale. She snooped in the spare room before I'd decided to show it to her because she was the sort of creature who went anywhere she pleased.

"What's all this?" she asked me.

"Some of Russell's mess."

She had a close look at a paragraph Russell had written on the wall while I gave her the shorthand version of Russell's condition.

She heard me out and said back something like, "Hmm."

"He went off with...Kelvin," I told her, "sometime in the night."

"I'm going to need you to help me find them."

"Where's your buddy?"

"Flu," she said. "I put in a call to your boss already. You're square for a couple of days." U-Dale gave my uniform a sneery once over. "Wear something else, all right?"

"I get a vote in this?"

She shook her head.

"Got to whack my hair?" I could do sneery too.

 U-Dale rolled up and blew the horn come morning. I carried Rusty off the screen porch and out into the back yard where I put him in the wading pool me and Russell used to use. It was about half full of smelly rainwater, but Rusty didn't appear to mind.

U-Dale didn't know about the trailer out at Del-Jo-Ray Acres.

In fact, she didn't seem to know much at all beyond Doug's name not being Doug. On the way over, I pressed her hard enough to earn a version of why they'd come. They worked for some guy in Tampa with money who had use for Kelvin's girl.

The door to the blue single-wide was standing open, and I let U-Dale go inside alone until she called out to me, "Hey." I found her in the cramped hall by the toilet.

I went as far as the bathroom door. "Got these from the sink"

She was holding a couple of small metal rods with copper wires sticking out. I didn't know what I was looking at.

"Blasting caps," she said.

"What are y'all doing?" Bike boy didn't miss a trick.

He was out in the yard on his banana seat. When he saw me, he said, "Oh, you," like he'd been hoping for a starlet.

"Talk to him," I said to U-Dale. "Got his nose in everything."

So showed him the blasting caps.

"Rico come through," he told her. "Kind of blows stuff up. Then some other fellow. Florida, like y'all."

"When?" she asked him.

"Little while ago."

"Tell me about this Rico."

"Went in there. Messed around a little. Come out and went on home."

"Where's home?"

Bike boy pointed more or less in the direction of Milwaukee.

"Want to show us?" U-Dale asked him. "Twenty in it for you."

That fellow threw his bike down like it had gone molten. "Shotgun." He was in the Chevy before me or U-Dale had moved.

Bike boy directed us deep into the countryside, well across the county line and out to territory where you'd see a house up by the blacktop and nothing behind it but weedy fields, weedy pastures, the occasional scraggly hedgerow. We turned off on a road the state hadn't put a plow on in a while, but that didn't seem to have much curbing effect on U-Dale's driving. She bar-relled along until we bounced sideways on the washboard when she stopped. She backed up a touch and then barrelled along some more. When the road gave out, U-Dale nosed her Chevy into a ditch.

We walked along a track between two runs of fencing, most of it collapsed. Bike boy supplied U-Dale with bits of Rico's biography as we went. It sounded like he'd started out burning his own stuff down to collect insurance and then hired out to burn stuff down for people who had insurance too. He got caught at that, locked up for a while, and came out keen on dynamite that he'd use to clear stumps and hollow out ditches. He even won a contract with VDOT to do some blasting for a road.

"Went nutty though." That's how bike boy put it. "Stayed mad about every little thing. You know how people get."

We did and both said so. Mad about every little thing had come to be the American way.

It seems Rico blew up a church bus while it was sitting empty one night and rigged a dumpster to go off at an Elk's Lodge just this side of Richmond. He was also thought to have exploded his brother-in-law's backhoe for reasons that weren't clear.

"They couldn't pin any of it on him," bike boy told us, "but everybody knew who to call if you wanted a thing blowed up."

The farm we were on had a collapsed house and a dairy barn with most of the roof tin gone, a shed that had maybe been for tobacco, and a hay barn in what appeared to be decent shape.

We proceeded the three of us up across a cow lot and over a rail fence to the hay barn where there was a heap of garbage – food cans and bottles mostly – and another heap beside it of what looked like workshop trash. Scraps of wood and lengths of wiring, rusty toggle switches, and tape spools and mess like that.

We found a tractor inside with a rear tire off and some implements for it that didn't appear to have seen use in a while. Back beyond them sat one of those rental pods with its roll door halfway down.

U-Dale squatted and had a look underneath. All she said was, "Hmm."

Then she scrabbled inside while I stayed out in the barn with bike boy.

"Got a phone with a signal?" U-Dale asked me from deep inside that pod.

I checked mine. "Yeah."

"Call the cops. Dead guy in here."

That was like Christmas morning for bike boy. He scrabbled under the roll door and scooted on inside. When I eased up for a look, I could see a man sitting against the back wall. He had one shoe off, and his naked foot was bloody.

First, we got a deputy who was the kind of knucklehead you'd expect that far out in the country. He was a beefy boy who knew how to wrestle drunks and break up squabbles but didn't know the first thing about dead folks beyond who to call in for a look.

He gave a shout to "Glen and them" who turned out to be a grumpy redhead and his partner, Keith.

They had the deputy write down all of our details, and it was like trying to teach Roman history to a dog. Glen and Keith quizzed U-Dale for a bit to get some read on who we were and what we were after, and I heard her tell them appreciably less than she knew. They finally cut us loose, and on the way back to Del-Jo-Rey Acres, bike boy dickered and bargained for thirty whole dollars in compensation and one of those gas-mart biscuits you heat in the microwave.

U-Dale was going to drop me in front of the house and pick me up in the morning, but once she'd pulled to the curb, she noticed my front door was standing partly open.

She went with, "Hmm," and reached down to her ankle where she pulled out a revolver. I stayed in the yard and let her go into the house.

She finally came to the front door and waved me on inside. I followed her to the kitchen where Russell was parked in his usual spot. His nasty clothes were on the floor, and he was wearing just his nasty diaper. There was a thing on the table in front of him. It turned out to be a toe.

HOTCHKISS

i

The man who hired me in Tallahassee had a daughter who was 'challenged', and he decided he ought to be sympathetic where it came to people like me. So he paid me nearly a going wage and yelled almost always at Homer even if I'd been the one who'd earned a dressing down.

We cut grass and trimmed shrubbery, blew anything that would blow, and worked mostly up in Killearn but sometimes down in Woodgate. I guess I was happy and satisfied. I was sure steadier than I'd been, but then Naomi came up to me in the Save A Lot and put pretty much an end to all of that.

I was reading a can of chunky soup. I read cans and I read boxes because I like to know if there's riboflavin in the food I eat. I'm not sure exactly what it does, but I'm convinced it's necessary.

"Hey," she told me and stood way too close, wouldn't let me ease away. She'd take two big steps for every little step I'd take.

"What are you doing?" she wanted to know.

I think I grunted at her.

When I was in Hotchkiss, I used to talk to people in a regular way. The patients. The doctors and nurses. The orderlies who held you down. I was probably something bordering on chatty. I'd talk about most anything and had a real gift for seeming keen on all the dreary stuff they'd tell me back. It must have helped that I was taking my pills and seeing Dr. Cox. We'd talk through my issues and work up lots of self-care strategies. She had a deviated septum. I liked to listen to her breathe.

When they first turned me out of Hotchkiss, I tried to keep the chatter up, but people seemed leery of me and not so eager to chew the fat, so I eased off, and it got to where I'd go great stretches only talking a little to Homer.

Then she came up and crowded way too close. "I've seen you," is what she said.

I thought she meant behind a Toro or on the skinny end of a rake.

"In a dream," she told me. "It was you in the moonlight wrapped up in a blanket." She shifted around for a look at the side of my head. "Yeah," she said. "It was you all right."

Even if I'd been properly medicated and not nearly so far from Hotchkiss, I still doubt I would have known what exactly to tell her back.

"I'm Naomi. I might look fourteen, but I'm not."

She didn't look fourteen at all but more like twenty-five trying for girlish. Short black hair with a ribbon in. A shift made out of corduroy. Shiny shoes with straps. Little white socks. A red plastic ring on her finger.

She stuck her hand out to shake mine. I couldn't help but take it. I've got no idea why I told her, "Doug."

She knew the boy who ran the tavern up around the corner, which said nothing good about her because it was one of those shabby spots with a pool table worn thin and a rowdy pack of regulars who bought their High Life in pitchers and argued about whatever came along.

The tavern guy fixed her a Jack and Ginger without her saying a thing.

A couple of boys at the end of the bar started pushing each other and raising a salty fuss, so the barman left us to yap at them for a while.

"It's like this sometimes," Naomi told me as she put a hand on my arm.

I figured she had to be playing me. Nothing else made any sense, but I couldn't work out what she might be playing me for.

Even though she drank four Jack and Ginger's, she stayed exactly the same. Two different boys came over and tried to chat her up. I couldn't blame them, a pretty young thing like her parked at the bar with me, but she moved them along about like you'd send cattle down a chute.

She spoke to me about the dreams she'd had with snakes and ghouls and spirits. I nearly told her how riboflavin would almost surely help, but instead, I just grunted and said I didn't sleep awful much myself.

"Come on." She took me by the hand, and we left the tavern together. Outside, she said she wanted to see my space (that's what she called it), so I walked her to the room I rented in a house a few blocks over. The woman who owned it liked to tell us it had been a swell street once back before the neighborhood went to pot and people around got trashy.

She lived downstairs in the front, and she peeked out when we came in. I said to her, "This is Becky, my sister's girl," because the truth was complicated and probably wouldn't have come out right.

Naomi told her, "Hey," and carried on like she was visiting from West Virginia. By the time she'd finished describing Wheeling, I half-believed her myself.

Up in my room, she talked astrology at considerable length before falling asleep in my easy chair. I threw one of my flannel shirts over her and piled into the bed. She was still there when the alarm went off, but she showed no interest in leaving, so I just pulled on my coveralls and went to work. I figured she'd get bored in a while and maybe head back to the Save A Lot where she'd tell some other fellow she'd seen him in a dream.

Instead, she was around when I got home, or was in the house anyway. She met me in the hall near the front door as I came in.

"Hiccup," she told me and led me into where my landlady lived.

I'd only ever been as far as the doorway when I paid the rent. The woman had the whole front corner to herself with the parlor and a side porch. Her decor turned out to be more cajun cathouse than I would have guessed. There were scarves on the lampshades and a stuffed, moth-eaten bobcat on the mantel. She had a coat tree with elaborate arms that reached almost to the ceiling, throw rugs piled three or four deep and splotchy dark red wallpaper that looked like Christmas wrapping.

"We were talking, us girls," Naomi said as she walked me through to a divan with my landlady half across it. She was face down with her knees both touching the floor.

"She had some kind of fit." Naomi coughed and gagged by way of describing it to me.

There was a pink lump on my landlady's head that had seeped blood just a little. It didn't look to me like something you'd get from pitching onto a divan.

"What do you want to do?" Naomi asked me.

I've never been good with decisions. I did know enough to go over and throw the bolt and set the chain.

Assorted valuables had somehow found their way onto my landlady's coffee table. Folding money and jewelry, three or four old wristwatches.

"Funny gal," Naomi said. "Used to sing at a club in Miami. Had some pictures she wanted to show me, but she only got that far."

I could have pressed her on it, I suppose, asked her what had really happened, but that hardly seemed worth the bother at the time. Instead, I helped her put all the stuff she'd piled up into a grocery sack. Then she wiped the doorknobs with a dinner napkin, and we went up to my room to work out who to call and what to do.

I had most of a pint of awful vodka in the drawer of my bedside table, and we drank that while Naomi described a few more of her dreams. One of them featured a Roosevelt and a Mandrell sister. They sang snatches of Scripture and both played claw-hammer banjos. Naomi said she'd had a waking vision about a fish with feet and some kind of gypsy woman carrying around a beet-red baby.

We didn't ever actually talk about my dead landlady downstairs and didn't make anything remotely like a plan. Naomi passed the night once more in my chair while I laid on the bed and wondered how it would feel to be back at Hotchkiss. They had people locked up in the blue ward who'd committed murder outright, the kind you do because of a kink in your brain. Those fellows couldn't be sorry for much and would never be mended or fixed. In the blue ward, they gave you a shower by shooting you with a hose.

Naomi woke up with buses on her mind. She'd made a trip once to Atlanta to see her cousin Percy. She pulled a face and told me, "Didn't go like I'd hoped," but even still she thought the bus ride there might be something approaching grand.

I knew better. I'd been on buses, but I packed some clothes in a sack anyway and then went downstairs with Naomi where we ducked into my landlady's place. She wasn't exactly how we'd left her. She'd crawled and squirmed a little, but she was cold when I checked on her while Naomi plundered through some drawers. She came away with a plastic sandwich sack holding three ladies' rings and another one that looked like it had some gravel in it.

"Why don't we call in once we get up the road?" she suggested. "Tell somebody about her?"

Of course, that wasn't something we ever actually did. Instead, we sold some of the jewelry to a woman Naomi knew and bought bus tickets with the money. We went all the way to Atlanta, but the ride was hardly grand even though our seats reclined and the air conditioner was working. Naomi told me along the way she had a clear sense this world was in a spiral. She said the lowly would rise and the mighty would fall before the land was scoured clean. Then she asked me for my birthday, and I picked a date.

"You're an enterpriser," was what she told me. "Goal-oriented, hard to please, but once you've set your mind to something, there's no way to put you off."

That wasn't me at all. I can be put off anything.

We went straight to Naomi's cousin Percy's house up in Atlanta, and once he'd opened the door and had seen who'd knocked, Cousin Percy tried to run, but we cut him off and cornered him in his kitchen.

He told Naomi he'd been high all the time and barely knew what he was doing. He said he didn't believe he ought to be held to account for stuff that old.

"What went on?" I asked her.

It was Percy who chimed in. "I was forward with the child," is what he said. He dropped his head and shook it.

Then Naomi described what exactly her cousin Percy had gotten up to with her, and it was tough to tolerate even before I found out she was eleven at the time.

I'd been a bad one to rage around before I got committed, before the treatments and the group talk and the pills. As a free man in Tallahassee, I'd largely kept myself in check, but I found Cousin Percy more than a little provoking. Almost before I'd even decided to, I was busting him to bits.

Naomi went through the house to see what Percy might have on hand while I stayed where I was and watched him twitch and groan. I knew even then I'd traveled a ways from walking behind a Toro, and I was aware there are places you go that you can't really come back from.

Naomi found a bit of money along with some kind of drug in little packets she figured we could sell. Naomi picked out better clothes for me and came across a lunchbox in Cousin Percy's closet, a pink one with horses on it that she told me had been hers. It had some stuff inside, and she added more from what we'd been collecting. Naomi even went a little misty before she beat Percy with a chair.

He had a Dodge in his carport, and we decided to hang around until after Atlanta's morning rush and then head on up the highway. I stretched out on the sofa in the TV room while Naomi stayed in the kitchen to acquaint her cousin with some of the dreams she'd had.

"Hey," she called to me after a while. "He's got a bone sticking out."

We left a milk jug full of water on the floor where Cousin Percy might could reach it, and Naomi took charge of his old Intrepid and drove us out of town.

"Where dirt is their drink," she said of Percy I think, "their food is of clay."

We stopped for gas up by Lavonia, and Naomi bought a phone. She said she'd call somebody to check on Percy, but I don't think she ever did. She told me she had a step-sister up in Spartanburg and wondered if we ought to swing by to see her. But then Naomi remembered they didn't get on and decided to drive on through.

Poppy is what she decided to call me when we were out and around. She wanted people to take me for her half-retarded uncle.

"You do," she told me, "look a little off."

I've long been oversized. There's six and a half feet of me. I've also got a dent in my head on account of a wreck I was in. So it wasn't like I could go around passing for ordinary.

We ate in a place at Gastonia, a cafe next to a motor lodge where a woman named Joyce with a brown incisor warned us off the food we'd ordered and directed us down the menu to stuff she thought we might survive.

"Where y'all headed?" she wanted to know when she brought our dinner rolls, and Naomi told her, "Baltimore" before adding we were coming from Alabama.

"Momma died down there."

"Oh, child."

"Burned up. Wasn't much they could do."

I couldn't tell how I figured in, so I just sat there looking sad until Naomi told Joyce I was her momma's brother and that I'd come back about half-ruined from the war.

"What one?" Joyce wanted to know.

She glanced my way like I could tell her, but, being ruined, I could only mumble and grunt.

"Ragheads and them," Naomi said.

Joyce allowed she'd figured as much.

"He does all right. Don't you, Poppy?"

I smiled like an idiot might.

"Could be he'll choke on the cutlet." Joyce hurried off to the kitchen to make sure they gave me something soft to chew.

For a first attempt, it wasn't too bad. We got free helpings of cobbler, and when we left, Naomi pulled me along by holding my little finger.

I didn't know where we were going, just knew I was a long way from the Save A Lot and was in precisely the brand of mess I'd been mowing yards to avoid. Even worse, I felt like I was awfully low on riboflavin and feared for how unbalanced and undernourished I might become.

"Where are we headed?" I asked Naomi once we were north of Charlotte.

"Know a woman up by Richmond. Feel sure she'll help us out."

That woman did help us out in the end, but she sure didn't seem to want to. I stood out on her front sidewalk while Naomi rang her bell, and it was easy enough to tell she wished she hadn't opened the door. Inside, she promised us three or four times that she wouldn't make any trouble and then pretty well begged us not to harm her cats.

It wasn't like they would have sat still for it. She had five of them, and they ran all over the place.

Her name was Marie, and she and Naomi had been neighbors sometime back. Marie was one of those people who sent holiday cards and worked to keep in touch, which meant Naomi was always well aware of exactly how to find her.

Marie called in sick for three days running. A friend came round to check on her the evening of day two. I hid in the basement. Marie had slipped into her bed, and Naomi was doing all the explaining. That woman stayed so long that I got bored down there and started poking through musty boxes of Marie's old stuff.

She had mildewed books primarily, lots of romance novels that were creased up like she'd read them several times. There were a half dozen pictures of a guy down there who looked a lot like Marie except for his droopy mustache and his hairline, and I found some buttons in a mint tin. They were brass and had ships on them. I imagined they'd look dead flashy once they were polished up, so I stuck them in my pocket and took a book as well that appeared from the cover to be about two shirtless men and a gun.

We weren't, as best I could tell, doing much useful planning. We were just eating stew and barbecue and keeping Marie upset. She was worried about her cats primarily but herself a little as well. I learned by sitting and listening that those two had been neighbors in Tennessee and that Marie had very nearly married a lanky man named Dennis, but they'd called it off just days before the wedding.

"We didn't get on," is how Marie told it.

Of course, Naomi wasn't about to let her get away with that, so she poked and tormented the woman about the true trouble with Dennis until Marie allowed she'd caught him doing unnatural things with a man.

We stayed with Marie for three full days, lived chiefly on stuff from her freezer, though she did have mushrooms in her crisper drawer. They're full of riboflavin. I ate all of them raw.

Naomi made a few calls on the phone she'd bought, and she'd always go out in the yard to do it.

When I asked her who she was calling, she'd just tell me, "Working a thing."

On the evening of our third day there, me and Naomi went out on the porch to decide what shape to leave Marie in. I was all for tying her loosely to one of the poles in the basement while Naomi sounded about half ready to crack her on the head, so we were out there talking through it as Marie climbed out a window and ran across the field off her back lot to her neighbor's place across the way.

Naomi wanted to drown some cats to punish her for it, but they wouldn't cooperate.

We pulled out in a rush and headed west, decided on the way to lay low in the foothills or the mountains and ended up renting a single wide in a half-empty trailer park. The place was hard beside a string of buggy mud holes, and people left us alone except for a boy Naomi cultivated, a wiry rascal who didn't appear to own a shirt.

Naomi was inspired by one of our neighbors to try her hand reading palms. She practiced on me. She was a good one for making a man think she found him beguiling. She could smile and trace your lifeline, tell you you had trouble ahead, and you wouldn't much mind because she was touching your skin.

She settled on Cheyenne for her fortune-telling name and set up in the roller rink grill where men came to eat fried bologna sandwiches and drink pitchers of flat beer while their kids and their wives were out on the hardwood under the disco ball. As a kind of bait, she started by reading my palm and telling me my future, did it with some volume and lots of tender touches and made it sound like I had all grades of stuff I ought to look forward to. Before she could finish, a slew of guys had crowded around to hear.

They were used to aimless chatter with their indigestion, so Cheyenne made for a vast improvement with her light touch and witchery, and it's hard to think her scoop-neck shirt didn't help things along as well.

There was no price on her readings, but she kept a pickle jar on the table that she'd salted with three fives and some singles crumpled up. She told those boys assorted mystical things and held their hands in hers until word got around, and the skating rink grill became the place to be.

Naomi was a terrible tease with those fellows, which hardly seemed fair or decent since about all they could do back was pull out their wallets and stuff cash in her jar. That became —

like all things where men are involved – a kind of competition, so soon enough it got to where Cheyenne was doing far better than all right.

There were three men in particular I felt a need to keep an eye on because they acted like shoving money in a jar would never be quite enough. One of them had gone in for hair plugs and a fresh set of too-white teeth. He'd decided he was a pure trial to resist and went around like having his way with Cheyenne was just a matter of time. Then there was a sad rancher named Hoyt who came to the rink with a couple of granddaughters.

He wouldn't have been much trouble to handle because he was old and balky, but a third guy took exception to the way Hoyt leered at Naomi and beat him to a bloody pulp one night. He went by Crow with his motorcycle buddies, but his wife only ever called him Lyle, and throttling people was how Lyle appeared to deal with just about everything. He'd object to something going on, would pause to weigh his choices, and then invariably settle on kicking some fool around.

Lyle's wife hauled their brood of children in an old Buick station wagon while he rode the kind of motorcycle a guy called Crow would ride. He ran with a gang that had *Gypsy Pagans* on the backs of their jackets and, like him, they were all a bit plump and gone to seed. Crow and his pals came across as the sort who largely lived for beer and a tussle, so I knew from the start when Lyle rolled in pretty much how things would go.

Noami managed the boy well enough for a couple of weeks. He kept telling her he wanted to see her alone away from the rink and out in the wild, and Cheyenne would usually read in his palm a future without her in it, which would cause Lyle to act like he enjoyed a tart girl there at first.

He didn't, of course. Men hardly ever do. It was just something to pretend about until he'd ground down her defenses, but then grandpa Hoyt suggested that Lyle leave Cheyenne alone.

Hoyt was probably pushing seventy with a balky hip and a dodgy shoulder, but Lyle went ahead and scuffed him up out in the parking lot. He didn't break any bones but closed one of Hoyt's eyes and laid the man's chin open. Cheyenne, good mystic that she was, told Hoyt what had happened to him as soon as he'd stepped into the grill.

She said to Hoyt anyway (and to me a little), "Crow."

I know instructions when I hear them, so I took on Crow as a job of work once I'd found him in the men's room putting jelly in his hair.

Lyle had one of those coifs that made him look like he was hanging upside down, which must have required an awful lot of hair slop and attention. It took him a while to notice I hadn't headed for a stall.

"What?" he asked me. Everything he came out with sounded like a threat.

I helped him fit in the trash can after a bit.

ii

I was doubtful Gypsy Pagans lived by much of a code since the bulk of those boys had things to do that didn't involve motorcycles. They had jobs and wives and weren't permitted to be louts all the time. Lyle, though, ran his life like he pleased and decided he'd be on a mission to make me sorry for what I'd done to him.

A few of his Gypsy Pagan brothers ganged up on me there at first. They caught me alone outside the rink, but their hearts weren't really in it. I'd picked up some tips at Hotchkiss from a blue ward guy with a kink in his brain, so I went at that bunch a lot harder than they were ready to go at me. They got deflated about it and saw fit to retreat.

Lyle wasn't much more effective himself. He made a few colorful threats and aired some unsavory pronouncements, but he was only big on swagger when we had some distance between us. I got the feeling he didn't much want to end up in a trash can ever again. I kept waiting for him to let the thing drop. I figured he'd eventually see the good sense of living with a smoldering feud. That way he could maybe slip up on me once I'd put him from my mind.

As it turned out, though, there was no cunning to him. Lyle's knack was for straight fury, and because he wasn't plucky enough to fool directly with me, he lashed out at his Gypsy Pagan brothers instead. He also had a battle with his wife one evening in the middle of the rink, and he shoved some teenaged boy around who'd rolled up in a Honda because Lyle didn't care for Hondas much on that particular night.

I stayed especially mindful of Lyle and his Gypsy Pagan brothers whenever Lady Cheyenne was working the rink cafe where she traced lifelines with her finger and said breathy things to men who'd grunt and wheeze and show her their molars back. Occasionally some guy with a couple of pitchers in him would try to paw her a little, and I'd have to help him find his way outside, but most of the men who came around were fairly well-behaved and preferred getting their futures told for a spot of folding money to dropping into the Top Hat to see some rough-looking girl try to dance.

The fellow who ran the skating rink grill was happy for the increased business, and all he turned out to need from us was the odd ten spot shoved his way. So we had a good thing going, and during time off I'd do the shopping and ride around in Percy's Dodge while Naomi would stay back at the house we'd swapped up to from the trailer and make, I had to think, her telephone calls.

From what I could pick up, Naomi had the hook in some rich guy down in Tampa, and she'd dial him most every day just to torment the man.

I'd usually end up in the Food Lion at a shopping plaza up the road and take my sweet time scoping out riboflavin. I probably got to be kind of a spectacle there reading cans and boxes, a big, hairy fellow with a dent in his head who must surely have struck folks as odd. That's probably why word about me filtered down to the wrong sorts of curious people.

I was reading a box of Rice-a-Roni when three Gypsy Pagans came at me. Since they were larded up and out of shape, I heard them wheezing along the aisle and was able to arm myself with a can of hominy and a can of pumpkin and managed to deliver some damage to those boys. The floor was slick, though, so we finally all went down in a heap. That's where they had the advantage, being blubbery and chunky, and they succeeded at laying their heft all over me.

That was their job, as it turned out, because here came Lyle to join us. Lyle anyway and a lady manager who wasn't about to tolerate her customers rolling around on the floor. Lyle said something demeaning to her, and she peeled off to make a call, so Lyle had to know time was short and county cops would soon be coming.

Consequently, Lyle made quick work of me.

"Give me some room," he told his boys, and they cleared a place big enough for Lyle to fit a boot through and kick me.

"Dead man," he told me and then kicked me one time further when I'm pretty sure the thing he said was, "Boom."

Then Lyle went sauntering down the aisle looking pleased with himself while his brother pagans rolled off of me and climbed the shelves to get upright.

Two deputies showed up shortly thereafter and quizzed me about that bunch.

"Don't know 'em," is what I went with. "Kept calling me Curtis. Must have thought I was somebody else."

The manager lady gave me a bag of frozen peas to hold against my dent because she'd decided it was fresh and tender, and I left the store that night feeling intensely itchy twitchy. I couldn't imagine Naomi would miss me much or even worry about me. That wasn't remotely the sort of thing she did. I knew she could tempt most any man to pick her up and take her places, so it seemed all right for me to be off by myself a bit.

I even slept all night in the car, had parked it back behind some old warehouses, and I woke up come morning all raw and tingly like Satan himself was scratching at me, so I stripped off my clothes right down to my skivvies and fetched Naomi's pink lunchbox out of the trunk of the Dodge because that had come to seem to me like just the thing to do.

Then I ran for a while. I can't say for how long and can't be sure of the ground I covered. I only know I woke up in a pile of wet insulation next to a half-built house feeling something close to ordinary.

Not quite ordinary enough to go back to Naomi, so instead, I stopped at an old farmhouse way out in the countryside. The grass was so high all around the place that it looked vacant and abandoned, but it turned out there was a man inside who was more or less alive. I got the clear sense his people had all left him to the Lord. He was stretched out in a smelly bed under a heap of smelly covers. He had cataracts like a hound might get. His eyes were both sky blue, and when he heard me come in, he looked the wrong way and just said, "Hey," and, "What?"

I found ham biscuits in a clump of foil on the kitchen table, and I picked most of the mold off of them and gave him one to eat. He had just enough teeth left to chew it. There was most of a pint of Ancient Age sitting on the toilet tank, and he squeezed my fingers when I brought him that as well.

I could tell from the pictures around the house he'd had a wife and what looked like a son, but he must have shed them somehow because he appeared to be down to nothing. We didn't talk. I pulled in a kitchen chair and sat for a time at his bedside. I opened cans of Vienna Sausages for him. He had no end of those.

I used his shower and his razor, found a shirt that nearly fit me, pants that I cinched up with a couple of safety pins. Once I was ready to go, I carried the man a can of Hormel chili, but it turned out he didn't need it. He'd gone to Jesus after all.

I stopped at his mailbox down by the blacktop to stick some paper behind the flag. I'd drawn an arrow on it and written "PASSED." Then I took a road that came out right beside a supercenter, and I stopped in to read a few boxes and some cans.

They usually leave you alone in a place like that, but my luck was poor, so that didn't happen.

"You're him, aren't you?" is what the woman said.

SANDALWOOD

i

She smelled worse than normal, and that's saying a lot. That gal went in for dollar store perfume, would spray a cloud in the room and walk through it probably three or four times a day. She liked her talcum and some kind of face cream that left her slick and shiny. Each of them was bad enough alone but close to toxic together.

"Wouldn't you know it," I remember telling myself when I found her on the rug.

I'd put a lot of work into Lois, had come at her from every direction. I'd been handy when she needed repairs, sympathetic when she wanted an ear to pour her maudlin rubbish into. I'd even flirted with her and let on I didn't mind that she was a smelly old bag.

She went so far as to "let" me kiss her once. I couldn't eat for two whole days.

I needed her place for keeping some stuff instead of squirreling it away downstairs. Every so often I'd get in a jam with exactly the wrong kind of people, and they'd come around ready to take whatever of mine they wanted to. I'd hold onto a little cash and a bit of dope to give them, but all the goods that really mattered would be stashed with Lois' upstairs.

I had my own key. I fixed her leaky taps and replaced her burnt-out lightbulbs. Every week or so I'd spend an hour putting her nasty kitchen right while suffering her to tell me all about her life as a chanteuse. I'd sometimes hold her hand in both of mine while she talked about some guy named Warren who Lois held out as her chief regret.

"Got on his knees," she'd tell me, "but I wasn't ready for

that." Sometimes she'd lay against me and blubber. When I went downstairs, I'd have to change my clothes.

So Lois dead on the rug just seemed like wasted effort to me. I assumed she'd simply collapsed like smelly old chanteuses will, but then I noticed stuff in the room upset. She wasn't clean, but she was tidy. There were drawers half-closed, and her Havana picture book was on the floor. I had a fresh look at the woman and spied the lump on the side of her head. It was all enough to set me scrounging around.

My cash was still in her freezer, and my pills were shoved back with her saucepans. I looked to be missing some watches and maybe a bracelet or two and went searching in the cubby where I'd stuck Uri's stones. I could see right away that they'd been pinched. I felt sick and had to sit down.

I dropped onto Lois' hassock, which put me right beside her.

"Who'd you let in here?" I wanted to know.

I checked her door. It didn't look pried. I could already picture Uri gripping my shoulder in Uri fashion. "Now, Viktor." He'd turn to Gleb who'd soften me up with a punch or six.

I figured I had maybe two or three weeks before Uri would come around after his stones, so I headed straight across the road to find out who'd paid a call on Lois. My neighbor over there wasn't one to miss a trick because he spent hours in front of his big bay window dipping snuff and noticing stuff. He had a large black woman who stayed with him days. She sat on the sofa reading her Bible and grousing about sinners, which explained the look I always got from her.

She let me in anyway, and I went straight to him. "Worried about Lois," is what I said. "Can't raise her. Seen her go out?"

"Thursday," he told me. "But she came back."

I looked grave. I'm good at that.

"The big one brought a girl." He described her in detail. The hair, the shoes, the corduroy shift. I knew exactly who he meant because I'd run across her before. We'd had kind of a thing for a little while. She used to tell me about her visions. People with their eyes pecked out, whole cities underwater, dogs gone feral, writhing balls of snakes.

The big one was Kelvin something, and he hardly talked to anybody. He had a room upstairs, and he came home days stinking of gasoline and grass. He wouldn't look at you unless you made him. I'd never raised more than a grunt.

I went up to his room. The door wasn't locked, so I walked on in. I hadn't seen the man in a while, but I could go stretches without seeing him, and I tried to remember if I'd even smelled him lately in the hall. There was a pair of socks under his bed and an empty bottle of rotgut vodka laying on his dresser along with the flap off a box of saltines where somebody – her I guess – had written a slew of girly stuff. She'd drawn a tree and maybe some kind of squirrel, had written the name Doug twice along with a phone number. I hid the thing in my shoe and then called the cops. They took me in like I'd figured because I'd found her and I had a sheet.

You probably make detective in Florida by eating four meals a day. They're all lumpy and short of breath, and the two I had were smokers who kept slipping out to chase down paperwork, they'd tell me, when they were only going for a butt. They'd leave files and notes and mess on the table that I'd sift through and read. I could see those boys had no idea about much of anything.

They were pulling jackets on everybody living in Lois' house, and it turned out Lois herself had done time for solicitation down in Broward but decades back when she was probably willowy and pricey. Kelvin had been in Hotchkiss up in Georgia for six years because he'd knocked around a neighbor girl and had tried to kill his parents.

They'd pulled paper on Naomi too. Last name Runyon, it turned out, and I helped myself to the sheet with all her details on it. I had it shoved down in my trousers before lumpy and lumpier could get back. They brought me coffee, like that's what they'd gone for, and then plopped back down to ask me a load of pointless stuff.

I checked on my own with Danny at the tavern, and he told me about Naomi and Kelvin sitting at the bar.

Danny couldn't say where she'd been living but pointed me to a fellow in a booth against the wall. It seemed Naomi had romanced him before she dredged up Kelvin, and I went over to try to talk to the man, but he was still wounded and fairly hot.

"That girl can make you do any damn thing." He looked like he might cry.

I called the number Naomi had written down and got a woman from up in Michaux, Virginia, on the line. Her name was Marie or something like it, and I told her I was a treasury agent. That usually throws them off since, if you were going to lie, you'd put yourself in maybe the CIA.

She wasn't talking much, this woman, and she got even quieter once I started on Naomi and her buddy. Real quiet. She'd say, "Uh uh," and not much else at all.

"She's not there right now, is she?" I had the sense to ask.

The woman said, "Yes, sir," but in a way that was kind of jolly like she didn't want to let on she was giving a treasury agent help.

I told her to stay calm and stuff like that, said I'd call the state police. Instead, I gassed up Lois' Bonneville and headed north.

I bought some proper clothes on the far side of Charlotte, a white shirt and a blazer. I stopped overnight in an interstate motel and passed the evening cleaning my gun. I was down to a .45. I had sold off all the others since it's gotten to where, with most capers, you hardly need to leave your house. You're better off with a phone, a laptop, and a silky smooth line of chat. So I had rust and gunk and fewer bullets than I wanted, but it was soothing to sit there with a rag and a can of WD-40, and after I'd gotten my pistol slicked up, I sharpened and oiled my snips a little too.

Michaux, Virginia, was one of those places that's nowhere much at all. It was probably a half-hour from Richmond and not close to anything else. I only needed to ask one fellow at a gas mart to get directed to the road I was after, and then I parked with a view of the house to see who was hanging around.

After an hour and no sign of anybody, I went up and rang the bell.

Marie had two night chains and what looked like a brand new deadbolt.

"What?" she asked me.

"We spoke," I whispered. "I'm treasury."

She told me with some vinegar, "State police never did come."

I muttered and swore, said that was just like them. "Are they still here?" I asked her.

She shook her head. "You got a badge or something?"

"It's treasury," I told her in a tone meant to convey that me showing up in new clothes should be enough.

"You could be anybody." She wasn't about to open the door.

"You're right." I could get what I needed from where I was. "Naomi Runyon and Kelvin? Big hairy guy?"

She nodded and then shook her head. "Doug," is what she said.

A cat tried to escape the house between the door and the jamb, but she informed it she wasn't in the mood and booted it away. Then she immediately got misty. "I'm a wreck." She told how she'd climbed out a window and run to a neighbor.

Then she spat out auto details because they'd been driving a brown Intrepid just like the one her mother's brother had owned.

"Georgia tag," she told me. "Said they were heading towards the mountains, but that could have been a lie."

I spent a day or two riding around in the hilly boonies between Charlottesville and the Shenandoah Valley where the population was sparser than I'd expected going in. I stopped at all the service stations and chatted up whoever I could, made Naomi out to be my sister who'd run off with a man of low character, and then I'd give the details on the Dodge.

"I'm afraid he'll harm her," is what I went with, and that was pretty much all I needed to say.

Nobody could tell me anything, but they promised to ask around because they had sisters or knew jackasses. Either one of them did the trick.

So I stayed in the area and hoped for the best. I picked up a college girl in a roadhouse without even working at it or meaning to. I'm sure it helped that she was half-lit, but I do have the hair and the square jaw, the abdominal definition, that seems to hit females just right. And I can back it all up with a line of talk that comes out suave without much strain, so they hardly have to be kegged up schoolgirls for me to work some magic on them.

She woke up crying, of course. I blame the motor hotel room chiefly. It must have looked a whole heck of a lot classier in the dark. Then she kept wanting to know how old I was and kept asking me what we'd done. The whole time I was driving her back to her car, she told me what she was usually like and how she ordinarily behaved.

I made her kiss me another time before I'd let her out. Of course, she blubbered about that too, the way they do.

It didn't take long at all before I caught a break. A guy with two pumps and a barbecue pit I'd given my number to phoned me up to say he had a boy who might could help me. He was back in the hillbilly part of things where people had every car they'd ever owned parked in their yards and most of the mowers they'd ever fooled with laying around as well.

The boy that man had called me about was sitting out front on his bike. Not a Harley or anything but just a bicycle he'd camoed with spray paint. His banana seat upholstery was black duct tape mostly, and he'd used the stuff for handlebar grips too.

He was one of God's peculiar creatures, was built like a child but might have been thirty. He was barefoot and in shorts, had on a t-shirt but wasn't wearing it in any regular way. He had his arms through the sleeves, but the rest of it was slung behind his neck.

"He said she's your sister," was how he opened up.

"That's right."

"She didn't say nothing about you."

"So you know her pretty good then?"

"Enough. Her and him was my neighbors."

"Was?"

He nodded and glanced towards the service station guy who was just inside behind the counter selling smoked shoulder to a man.

"He says you'll pay," bicycle boy told me.

The service station guy must have heard him and so shouted our way, "Did not."

"I can take you where they were staying."

He wanted twenty. I offered ten. Five up front and five when we got there, which he was fool enough to agree to.

The place was a comedown even for Kelvin, and he'd been living in a room with peeling paint and mildew for decor.

"How long they been gone?" There wasn't much to look at, just a sofa and a bed.

That boy didn't want to talk to me because I'd not paid him in full, so I pulled out my snips and offered to lop off a finger joint or something, and I think even he could tell my hardware was oiled up and looked ready to get some use.

Those tin snips were a Uri thing. He carried his pair instead of a gun because he had Gleb his Belarussian ready to beat whoever required it, which left Uri free to swan in and threaten people with his snips. I saw him amputate a toe once. A fellow had gone in arrears with Uri, and Uri would only renegotiate once that guy was nine toes to the good.

Gleb pulled off his shoe and his sock and then held his foot so Uri could find a toe he liked and snip it. The man yelped and wailed but not a lot, and I thought he'd bleed more than he did. Uri told him about the new terms as he wiped his snips with a hanky. I want to say that nine-toed fellow might have even thanked him. It must have felt like a reprieve since, as a young man, Uri had been known to prefer a machete. He'd told me once snips were elegant, and I'd decided he was right.

I found out Naomi and Kelvin had been gone for several days.

"Ran into trouble with some motorcycle boys or something. They sent Rico over, but he didn't feel good and left. You just missed him."

"Who's Rico?"

"Blows stuff up."

"Was he here for that?"

"Prolly."

"Where's he stay?"

I got by way of response a quarter-hour of directions.

Rico lived in a barn out and away from most humans, and I couldn't drive anywhere near it but had to walk through two pastures and work my way around a mudhole to close in. Even still, he didn't see me coming until I was all the way inside.

He stayed in one of those big moving boxes shoved back behind a tractor. The door was up, and he was sitting in the only chair in the place having what I'll call breathing difficulty.

Such difficulty, in fact, that he didn't bother to ask me who I was and what I wanted but instead just told me, "Something's wrong," like maybe I'd come to help him.

I got down to business and acquainted him with all I wanted to hear, but he went on struggling to draw breath and pretty much ignored me. So I took out my snips the way Uri would, pulled off a boot and a sock.

"Give me a name."

"Rico."

"Not you, man. Who you working for?"

He finally told me, "Lyle," and described a roadhouse where I'd find him. He kind of laid out where it was, but it took him so long that I'd clipped a toe before he could finish up. To his credit, he hardly seemed to notice but got busy instead shifting off of his chair and piling up on the floor.

"Something's not right." He just wouldn't let it go.

"Yeah, isn't that the way," I told him. I couldn't even find a decent rag in that place to wipe my snips off with.

I headed to that roadhouse while the directions were fresh in my mind, but there were just a few hayseeds around and a woman named Penny back of the bar who had her shirt about half unbuttoned so she could show off her red brassiere.

"What'll it be, hon?" Penny was that kind of gal.

I had a beer and a bump while I asked her about Lyle.

Penny leaned in to tell me on the low low, "Bunch of dopes, him especially."

She'd been married to one. Then she'd married a plumber, she told me, and after him she'd lived with a boy who did framing when there was any work around.

"On my own now." Penny winked my way and refilled my beer on the house.

She let me know that Lyle would be coming in on a blue and tan Indian Chief, which was enough to allow me to wait up the road and lay for the guy in Lois' Bonneville. Soon enough those motorcycle boys started rolling up and straggling in. Lyle only showed after a while. He was riding on his own, so I eased right out and nudged him into the ditch.

He was angry about it, naturally, but his bike was laying on him, and the hot parts of the engine were burning him through his pants.

"Christ, buddy!" he told me while he lifted and pushed but didn't really get anywhere.

"That boy you want to blow up," I said. "He's the one I'm after. Him and that girl."

Lyle pushed his motorcycle some more. He didn't want to tell me anything, but that was chiefly the roughneck in him, and once his muffler started blistering his leg, he changed his tune pretty quick.

"Skating rink," he said and then supplied me with more country directions like if I went past the place where the Sunoco used to be, then I'd have gone too stinking far.

"Help me." He was just about crying.

So I sort of did, aired an opinion anyway. "It's a wonder," I told him, "you folks around here ever get any damn where."

I only found that skating rink after some serious wandering around, but it proved a cinch to locate Naomi because she was working a play inside. A pack of men had congregated at the table where she was sitting. She was holding some boy's hand and telling him every lively thing that lay ahead for him in his life. I recognized the look on his face well enough. He was primarily aroused.

I hung back to scope out her big hairy buddy, but I didn't see him anywhere and so eased on up to join the clutch of men beside the table. She was reading cards and telling the boy beside her that he was in line for some farming equipment he'd soon land at a decent rate.

"So answer your phone," she suggested, "and talk to people you might not want to."

He told her shirtfront mostly that he would.

Then she sniffed the air like she was getting a whiff of something upwind. She blubbered and pointed my way, said I was a man who'd used her poorly.

"He took me!" she said, kind of wailed it really and came off as wrecked and upset.

Naomi announced through tears that I'd forced myself on her at a Presbyterian church where she'd gone to pray for an uncle of hers who'd died in a sawmill mishap. She went into some detail about how I'd cornered her in the narthex.

"He took me," she told them, "in a house of God."

Those boys gave me a hard once over. I had to suspect they could picture themselves taking the girl as well, but they hadn't because they wouldn't, and yet there I was and had.

I tried to say she was mistaken and that I'd never been in a narthex, but those boys were anxious to do a turn for Naomi and so knocked me over and held me down.

Then she loosed tears, streams of them, and I came to understand that I was maybe in a spot of trouble. She said she was only just starting to feel alright and there I was in her life again.

Naomi was a talent. I had to give her that. And those boys were ready to do about anything she wanted.

One of them went to his truck for rope, and then a bunch of them tied me up. Three of them took me in a van way out into the country where they hauled me down alongside a pond and lost (praise Jesus) their nerve. They spent a while trying to find the sand between them to do me in, and I concentrated on coming off full of regret and pitiful. If there'd been a few more of them out there, something approaching a mob, I would have expected to end up plugged down in the silt and mud. It was a hard lift, though, for three regular guys to set their decency entirely aside. Instead, they elected to kick me around and air some hard opinions. Then they all three went back to the van and left.

It was dark by that pond but for a touch of moonlight. Two rabbits and a fox came through. The more I tried to work my knots loose, the tighter they all got. My hands were hurting from no blood much and one of my knees was giving me fits when a boy showed up in the early morning with a fishing pole. A real boy, not just some hayseed roughneck. He looked maybe ten years old.

"Hey," he said like he saw men tied up on pond banks all the time.

I went with, "Morning. Sure glad to see you."

"What are you doing?" He baited his hook with white bread from a sack.

"Getting married," I told him. "Buddies playing a trick. You know how that goes."

He nodded. He spat and told me in time, "All right."

"Got a knife?" I asked him.

He nodded again. He tossed his line out and watched his bobber.

"They're not coming back," I told him. "All part of it, you know?"

He got a bite and caught a bream about the size of his palm. He worked it off the hook and tossed it back.

"I'm never getting married," he told me.

I nodded and said, "All right."

After maybe an hour of that sort of thing, he finally cut me loose. He'd kept a couple of crappie by then and I'd learned he played the banjo but only a little.

"Where's the road from here?" I asked him.

He pointed pretty much at the sun.

A Jesusy woman in a rusty station wagon picked me up on the blacktop. She shared quite a lot of scripture with me, stuff like "The living know they'll die, but the dead know nothing," and "Because of the Lord's great love, we are not consumed, for his compassions never fail."

She was jonesing for a cigarette and had stopped for me hoping I'd have some.

"Quit years back," I told her. "What exactly's a narthex?"

I don't think she knew because all she said was, "Resist the devil, and he will flee from you."

Lois' Bonneville was still in the skating rink lot, but somebody had poked a hole in one of the tires, so I was trying to figure out the jack when a fellow in a cowboy hat came rolling up to watch me put on my doughnut. He was driving an ancient Camry with at least four dachshunds in it and so much nose smear on the windows I don't know how he could see out.

Then I couldn't locate that trailer park where Naomi and Kelvin had stayed, and I rode around lost for probably an hour before it showed up in the wrong place and on the wrong side of the road. I drove all through it and finally came across banana-bike boy who was trying to get away until I swung my door open and knocked him over.

"Come on, mister," he said.

I put a foot on him to hold him down. "They been back?"

He looked mystified until I used my hands to describe Naomi.

"Naw," he told me. "Ain't seen them."

"Makes this a funny place to blow them up."

"I guess," is what he went with.

"Anybody else been around?"

Banana-bike boy nodded. "Rent-a-cop lady." He sort of knew where the rent-a-cop office was and so pointed nowhere much and told me, "Town."

Town wasn't a place of any size, maybe three blocks total, and it was one of those bergs that had seen most of its store-fronts empty out. Instead of soaping the windows, they'd put up posters advertising local attractions, an old-timey waterwheel, a petting zoo, some sort of Civil War/Putt-Putt attraction called *Dixie Storyland.*

The office for Assurance Security was a little ways down the block, and when I stepped inside, the woman there told me, "Barry's gone for a muffler."

I have to think I didn't look enlightened.

"You here about the job?"

I shook my head. "Looking for a woman. Told she works for you."

"What woman why?"

"She turned up in a will. Got a piece of cash coming her way."

She looked mildly doubtful and suspicious, so I hit her with a dose of the old charm.

"Justin, by the way." I offered my hand. She put her fingers within reach. I took them.

"Lori," she told me and gave me a squint. "Haven't I seen you at The Barn Door?"

That had to be some honky-tonk. I snapped my fingers. "Thought so," is what I said.

She named a bunch of local people to find out if I knew them, but I told her I'd been keeping to myself for the last little while since my wife passed away.

She made sympathetic noises and rubbed my arm. Lori struck me as one of those women who divided her time between the Stairmaster and tequila shots.

"What is it y'all do exactly?" I picked up a pamphlet off her desk, opened it, and made to be enthralled.

"Like it says – we keep an eye on what you can't."

She wasn't really my type. Too wiry and way too much tanning parlor. But there was hardly a limit to what I'd do to keep Uri off my back.

She got a radio check from one of her troops, ten-foured him and everything, and then turned back my way. "Older lady?"

I took a chance and nodded.

"Probably Dottie."

"She working today?" I asked.

"Kind of on leave."

"Got a home address for her?"

"Who you with again?"

That seemed like the perfect time to hit her up for lunch spots. She named three or four, including a swanky new place where a bank used to be.

"Grill right in the table. You cook your own meat on it. That's how they do it over in Mongolia."

"Yeah," I told her, "and Arkansas."

We had a laugh. I said, "Come on. Let's grill some meat. My boss is paying."

She hesitated but in a coy I'm-coming-eventually sort of way.

She drove us in her car to the restaurant where the bank had been, and a couple of HVAC boys and us were the only people there. They were busy installing exhaust pipe because table cooking is extra smokey.

I insisted we have a couple of drinks, some Mongolian concoction that tasted of lemonade and gin. Then they brought us raw lunch that we grilled at the table and so soon enough smelled like we'd been smoking a goat.

Lori was the sort who took very little priming to open a spigot of chat. I asked her a thing or three, and off she went. I nudged her to Dottie when I could and got rewarded with piecemeal details. Lori told me Dottie's husband, Russell, had been a good hire before his stroke.

"Real particular," is how she put it. "Dottie, not so much."

Lori also had me understand that Dottie was a wrinkled and pear-shaped woman, which were features of life, Lori informed me, she was personally warring against.

"Feel that." She made a muscle. I felt it. It was the size of an egg, and that's when she looked at me and I looked at her, and I guess we both knew what we were in for.

It did seem possible pillow talk might help fill a gap or two, so we shared a last Mongolian cocktail by way of capping off our lunch and then went to the car where we had a preliminary grapple. Lori drove us to her place, a tiny apartment she hadn't tidied up in probably half a year. It wasn't dirty necessarily but more in the way of a girly mess with outer clothes and underthings draped everywhere you could drape them and stuffed rabbits scattered pretty much all over the place.

She told me before I could ask her, "Always had a thing for bunnies." She was already shucking her shirt by then.

Lori wasn't one of those women who felt the need to lay down ground rules and explain to a man how it was mostly liquor and luck and didn't mean anything to her. She was rail-thin, plenty of sinews and bony hollows, and she caught me so flush with an elbow while in the throes of passion that I feared I might need a suture or two.

Sex was a Greco/Roman thing with her. You rolled around. You came violently together and then you moved apart. After about three minutes, you rolled around some more. A cat jumped onto the bed near the middle of our third try, and she pitched it into the closet without even breaking rhythm.

It turned out Lori didn't leave a lot of gaps for pillow talk, but I tried to make the most of what I got. I mined a fair bit of piffle out of her that I didn't want or need, but I also heard about Dottie and some big, hairy guy running naked that Dottie was helping police from Miami or somewhere try to track down.

Then Lori was reminded of an old boyfriend of hers who'd not held up, but she told me they'd had a wild time in the day attempting all sorts of stuff. She described to me a couple of their more acrobatic exploits before insisting, naturally, we have a go at one. I made an effort to be game with the girl but ended up dropping her onto the floor.

She finally gave me a location for Dottie, not an address but enough to work with. "Lives out towards Lamar near the paint store." Then she yanked my pud and said, "One more."

Lamar turned out to be a part of town and not just a street I could ride on. As neighborhoods go, this one had been around for a while and looked it. A lot of brick ranchers with bushes in front and neglected stuff in the yards. A few people had prettied up their lots with flower beds and cement geegaws, but I got the feeling most everybody else was too busy holding two jobs for that.

I went up and down every street and finally spied a Ford Fiesta with *Assurance Security* stenciled across the back glass. It was parked in the driveway of a brick rancher with a half-dead dogwood tree in the yard and an upside-down push mower in the ditch.

I knocked but couldn't raise anybody. Nobody in the actual house anyway, though some guy came out to talk at me from the road.

"She's not home," he said. "Russell neither."

"Any idea when they'll be back?" I left the porch and walked his way.

He had a slew of tattoos leaking out from his collar and cuffs. He even had tattooed finger joints and ink behind one ear, which came off as peculiar because otherwise he looked like he'd do your taxes.

"What do you want?" he asked me.

"To talk to…" I pointed at the house.

"Why?"

"Private matter."

That didn't appear to work for him.

"Know when they'll be back?"

"A while, I guess."

He was like a lot of people I'd been running across in the world. They showed up ill and went downhill from there. There was a time when I would have busted him up rather than retreat, but working with Uri and them had wised me up a little. "I'll try her later," I said and left the place.

I climbed into Lois' Pontiac, drove three or four blocks over, and then went walking until I'd found a way to slip into Dottie's back yard. There was a nasty little wading pool with a white duck floating in it and knee-high weeds and bushes up against the house. So it was a chore to get to the windows, but I finally found one with the lock half busted and with a sash I could slip my blade under and pry.

That house smelled of fry oil and yesterday's socks. The lone bed wasn't made, and the bathroom looked like somebody had flat torn it up, but it was the back playroom that pretty much stopped me cold.

The far wall was all scribbled up and covered in string and crap, and there were packing boxes on the floor and no furniture at all except for a folding chair with a pink lunchbox parked on it. The writing might have been Hebrew, and string was running nearly all over the place.

You can't truly ever know about people. That's what I'm always telling myself. You can stand there chatting in a checkout line with a guy who's a cannibal at home, but how are you going to figure it out if you don't look in his freezer?

So I was having random thoughts like that when I caught sight of a little ziplock bag taped up to the wall. It was situated between a crushed beer can and the husk of a cicada and had string going to it from six or eight different spots. I stepped straight over and plucked the thing free. They were Uri's stones sure enough. The air around me was suddenly sweeter to breathe once I had salvation in hand.

I heard a key in the front door, so I bailed straight out the window and landed in some leggy, sprawling bush. I was too busy working free to notice her behind me until I felt the bore of her pistol on my neck.

"Jesus, stinky," that gal said, "what the hell are you doing up here?"

I could only half see her but that proved enough. How are you going to forget that hair?

U-DALE

He was working security for a woman with a gnarly ex and a string of trashy boyfriends. There were places she could go that Jerry wasn't allowed to follow, and he'd heard from some buddy I'd been solid before I shot a guy reaching for his phone.

When I met him for coffee, I expected to get quizzed up. Instead, Jerry treated me to his ragged history with booze.

"I'm all right for now," is how he capped it.

I liked the way that sounded and told him, "I guess I'm some of that too."

His client, Sue, ran a dental supply house that she'd wrangled away from her ex, and the ex was aggressively unhappy about it. He kept making threats and staging confrontations and would have been enough alone to keep me and Jerry busy, but Sue made a habit of running around with other dodgy men.

She'd latched onto an underwear model named Bryce about the time I caught on. He was sculpted and pretty and owed money to all the wrong people for all the wrong reasons. He was also gay sometimes and had a boyfriend from Boca who'd show up every now and then to pitch a fit and make a scene.

I'd never worked that sort of gig before. I'd been a street cop and then, briefly, a gun-happy detective, so I was obliged to adjust my thinking and tweak my whole approach. Jerry proved to be just the guy to help me along with that. He'd established a kind of beachhead among the peccadillo set. It wasn't just Sue. His clients generally had randy whims and itches, hobbies up to and including felony assault and negligent homicide. Jerry was who they'd call to make the bother go away.

We had a reliable repeat offender named Byron down in Tampa. Jerry had been on retainer with him since well before he hired me on. I'm fairly sure the stuff Byron got up to wasn't authentically criminal, but it was certainly kinky and tawdry, and he wasn't about to give it up. Byron licked teen girls but always only did it with their permission. He preferred them pubescent, favored brunettes, and he'd swab their armpits and the backs of their knees. Not even for very long. As lickers go, Byron was decisive and efficient.

He had a couple of agents in the field recruiting talent for him. One was a good-looking kid named Lance with a pricey sneaker habit and the other was Kathleen who'd graduated from getting licked herself. She didn't seem to have suffered much for it and had stayed on friendly terms with Byron who paid her well to round up girls and bring them to his house.

The first time I saw Byron indulge himself he was on his patio with his nose shoved in some child's pit. She didn't appear to mind the attention and shortly ended up with a Fresca that she carried into the shallow end like nothing had gone on.

Jerry explained our job was chiefly to help Byron keep a lid on things. He'd made his money selling reclaimed platinum from catalytic converters, and Byron had underwritten the cost of bringing opera singers to Tampa to perform at an auditorium he'd paid to renovate. So the man had civic standing, and he wanted to stay well thought of without giving licking up.

The bulk of our working hours were divided between Byron and Sue. We had a client named Gunther for a while, but he got killed by an alligator somebody he'd wronged had been careless enough to leave loose in Gunther's house. Work for Byron was steady while Sue flared up just every now and then. She'd sometimes get back with her ex but never for more than a week or two. Then they'd fight, and Sue would reel in some chiseled man/boy to console her.

Sue's taste in men was reliably deplorable, and she finally crossed a line with a guy named Viktor, a small-time grifter and chiseler from up the coast. He was a strapping specimen who wore a puka necklace and used sandalwood cologne that, by the reek of it, he applied with a bean sprayer. Sue came across him in a hotel bar and brought him home for an entire weekend. She informed us he had remarkable technique.

"What's that mean?" Jerry asked me later.

I laid it to part cologne poisoning and part basic anatomy.

Sue gave Viktor a house key decidedly against our wishes and permission to come and go from her place as he pleased. We'd poked around by then and knew Viktor had a sheet for larceny and had somehow gotten out from under a couple of sexual misadventure charges. So we were already leery of him long before he brought Uri around.

Uri was the closest thing on the Florida gulf coast to a Corleone. He had fingers in every shady thing that went on. His people had been Russian, and while Uri still consorted with various eastern bloc types, he came off as fully American and spoke the brand of Florida English that's half Confederate colonel and half Miami Jew. He was an *oy vey* and *I swanee* sort of guy.

Uri dressed mob casual and could pass for a gentleman, but he was notorious for using tin snips as an instrument of persuasion. He'd clip the occasional finger or odd toe. It was his way of being emphatic when nothing else would do.

Jerry tried to make Sue understand that Uri and Viktor were out to fleece her and that she ought to stick all her valuables off in a vault somewhere. Sue, though, refused to believe him, insisted she had a nose for people. She told us she didn't much care about the stuff she owned anyway. A good thing as it turned out since Viktor made off with a fair bit of it, including a couple of raw emeralds Sue had forgotten she even owned. Then Viktor packed up his technique and went back to Destin or wherever. Sue stayed sad for most of an entire day but then glommed onto a lifeguard. His name was Kai, and he called everybody *Yo*.

So it seemed like Uri was out of our lives, sandalwood Viktor too, and we went back to paying the lion's share of our attention to Byron who along about then had fallen under the spell of an odd creature who quite plainly wasn't even an actual girl.

She was female certainly but nothing like fourteen. We'd find out in time that she was twenty-seven. She had a page-boy cut and usually wore a corduroy shift with buttercups on it. The shoes she favored were patent leather with silver buckles, and she went in for the kind of white, frilly socks babies off to get christened might wear.

Aside from the surface details, she made no attempt at all to persuade. She talked to Byron like a woman while looking sort of like a girl, and she succeeded at getting to him in ways real little girls just couldn't. She was even up for licking Byron back.

She went by just Kiki and made it tough for us to find out who she was. We kept a running tally of everybody who came and went from Byron's, and Jerry put me to work on Kiki who'd claimed to be a friend of a friend of a girl in the pool named Amber, but Amber told me she didn't know her and doubted she had a friend who would.

It proved impossible to get any useful details out of Kiki herself because she was cagey and elusive and had a knack for talking a lot without saying really much of anything. Worse still, Byron discouraged us from any sort of serious digging because he wasn't by nature careful and she was pushing his buttons pretty good.

That took no great insight on her part. She could see what Byron wanted and supplied it in the form that he required. He'd swab her, and she'd dare to swab him back.

"I might just love her," Byron said to Jerry one day out of the blue. "Sometimes," he confessed, "I don't even want to lick her."

It didn't seriously matter to us if Byron got hooked up with some phony teen. She was well north of statutory, and if she only loved his money, she'd be in a fine tradition down around where we lived. We did, however, feel duty-bound to check her out nonetheless in case she was working for maybe the feds and trying to put Byron in some trouble.

She claimed to be Kiki Evans from down around Mobile, and she tried at first to say she was sixteen, but her heart wasn't really in it, so she soon allowed she was twenty-two and said she'd left Alabama because her daddy had taken undue liberties with her.

The only ID she ever showed me was from some Georgia community college, and she always came and went from Byron's house in a local cab. I ended up having to follow her home way up north around Azure Estates where she was staying with a boy who knew her as Ellen. He told me she worked as a legal aid.

I managed to strike up a conversation with him at a Waffle House near his place where I made out to be new to the area and in need of local input. His name was Ted, and he was a friendly sort – not to say a sap – who kept wishing I could talk to his girlfriend because she knew every little thing. They'd met in a Publix. She'd come right up and told him she felt like she knew him, believed maybe that they'd been joined together on some other plane.

"Stuff like that never happens to me."

Ted told me that twice, and I believed him. He was pleased to rattle on about his Ellen. The walks they took, the chats they had. In a whisper, he confided that the sex they enjoyed was almost exclusively tantric.

"We get up to things," he told me, "but mostly in our heads." He laid that off to Ellen being Catholic.

I followed Kiki to a different place a couple of evenings later. Different apartment. Different sad-sack guy. From the peck I saw him give her, I didn't doubt she was being Catholic with him too.

So we still didn't know exactly who she was when she had her blowup with Byron. He got crossways with her. Byron couldn't explain exactly how, and she raged and pouted and left the house once she'd announced that they were finished. Byron mustered the dignity and self-respect to endure her absence for two days before he called us in to tell us, "I want her back."

Jerry ended up enlisting a cop buddy to run prints he'd pulled off a White Claw can. She'd been picked up once for solicitation, and she wasn't an Evans from Alabama. Her name was Naomi Jean Runyon, and she was from some Georgia wide spot. She'd done a semester in Tallahassee where she still got mail in a box. Byron gave us one of his Chevys to drive. They'd come with some outfit he'd taken over, and he handed Jerry two inches of money to hold us until we found the girl.

If we didn't find her and grab her, he made it clear, we shouldn't bother to come back.

This Naomi certainly made an impression everywhere she went. They knew her around campus in Tallahassee, in the local shops and the bars, but nobody had seen her lately. Once we'd moved out and away from the college to the seedier parts of town, folks there allowed they knew her too, and she'd been around more recently. One of them directed us to a tavern where the bartender made himself useful.

"Kind of an operator," he said. He didn't know where she lived, but he'd gotten wind of some trouble she helped stir up and directed us to a boarding house two streets down and a few blocks over.

"Lady turned up dead. Maybe fell over." He sucked his teeth. "Or maybe not."

There was a single strand of police tape across the lady's door. Jerry thought about calling for clearance, but the door in question was the swollen sort that didn't actually catch, so instead, he shouldered it open, and we walked on in.

The place was a mess, cop leavings mostly but some questionable decor too. The drawers were all out and the closet doors open. They'd removed a square of rug and appeared to have picked through everything else while dusting for prints all over. Jerry put in a call to a Tampa cop he knew who got into the system and reported back there was interest in a tenant, a guy named Kelvin with a history of violence who'd been in the bughouse for a while.

We had a look in his room upstairs, but there wasn't much to see, and then we went back to the tavern to check again with that bartender.

"Big and hairy," he told us. "Some kind of dent in his head."

And that's how it went for us. We couldn't know it then, but things would never get faster or slicker or better. Jerry would check every day or so with Byron to gauge the level of his interest since there were fresh girls showing up at his Tampa house all the time. Like the bulk of men, though, Byron simply had to have the one who'd thrown him over. The cost of bringing her to him didn't matter to Byron, so we kept sniffing along the trail.

Two inches of money can last a while, and we had nothing pressing. Sue was off in Bilbao with a young man of Moroccan extraction and unspecified technique.

Along the way, we established that Naomi Runyon had family near Atlanta. Druid Hills specifically, and the shabby house we found there had been some kind of crime scene too.

Jerry managed to wave down a radio car, and the cop inside told us the owner was busted up but still hanging on.

"Got suspects?" Jerry asked him.

He shrugged like he couldn't be bothered to know. "Major creep. Might have been anybody."

We located the creep and paid him a visit. He was plastered up to a fare thee well and had drain hoses coming out and tubes going in. One eye was uncovered, but it was runny. Even still he seemed aware that we were there.

"Percy, right?" I left it all to Jerry.

The man-made a noise, a squeak.

"Sorry for your..." Jerry scanned him up and down. "Maybe you can help us out."

He squeaked again, which sounded to Jerry affirmative enough.

"Looking for Naomi." We had a mugshot for some drug thing, and Jerry showed it to the guy.

He had a violent spasm and was still at it when a nurse came in to tell both of us, "Hey!"

We went back to Percy's house in the dark and let ourselves inside. There was a busted up dinette chair in the kitchen and dried blood on the linoleum, a stack of mail on the counter that Jerry went through. He found Percy's insurance bill with his auto details on it. Since Percy's car shed was empty, Jerry called one of his cop buddies and gave him the VIN. That Dodge had been ticketed in a fire lane three days earlier in Virginia.

We stayed the night in a motor hotel just outside Atlanta. It was next to a shopping plaza with a Rack Room and a liquor store, and for some reason, that's where Jerry decided to tumble off the wagon. He had a flagrant history, ordinarily with rum, but Jerry turned out to be the sort who'd drain your jug wine in a pinch. He'd master the itch for stretches, but when he gave up, he lapsed hard.

I had the room next door and heard him knocking around in the small hours. He came out in the morning with a scab on his nose, and he told me he'd tripped on the bathroom rug.

We drove to Virginia. I drove to Virginia.

"Got a stomach," Jerry told me. I stopped about every other hour so Jerry could throw up.

I'd soon figured out what was going on, chiefly from how he stank, and I felt like the man was permitted a relapse every now and again. He'd be sick for a day, I told myself, and then saddled with regret and probably dry for a decent stretch after that.

We stopped at the county police office outside Chesterfield, Virginia, where Jerry took the lead in chatting up a couple of detectives. He always wore his union pin and carried his old credentials, and cops are borderline foolish about helping each other out. So we soon found out that Percy's car, an old brown Dodge Intrepid, had been up around there just a little while back.

"Those two stayed with a woman. Hostage thing," is how that county cop put it. He even called the lady and made an appointment for us. We were waiting out at her place when she rolled up from work. She was plump and nervous to the point of maybe ruin.

"I know they would have killed me," is what she told us. Her name was Marie.

Jerry walked her through her whole ordeal with Naomi and her manfriend, a hulking, dented fellow she called Doug.

We had a photo to show her from his Hotchkiss file – Kelvin Fergus Mackie. He was maybe nineteen when the picture was taken, but you couldn't miss that dent.

"That's him," she told us. "What did they do?"

"Made a mess of a fellow in Georgia," is what Jerry decided to tell her, and he caught Marie right when she started to quiver and before she could manage to fall.

As bad as it was with the vomit and all, that was Jerry's last good day. He'd retire nights to his motel room with a quart or two from somewhere. He was a quick and joyless drinker, would little more than pour it down and then show up in the morning looking more barked up and baggy. I tried to talk to him about it once or twice, but he'd just grumble and show me his gun.

Since I couldn't call in favors like Jerry could and didn't have his nose for details, it was a dead lucky thing we strayed across that brown Intrepid on the two-lane. We were scouting around well west of Chesterfield when I saw the Georgia tag.

"Might be them," I said to Jerry.

It was too close to liquor o'clock for Jerry to manage much beyond, "Urrghh."

By the time I'd turned around and located that Dodge again, the guy with the dent was parking in front of a Food Lion. He went in, and I waited a few minutes and then went in as well to find him halfway up the vegetable aisle reading a can of something. When he put that one back, he picked up another, and read it for a bit. He eventually left without buying anything.

We followed him for a while longer. He seemed to be just riding the roads. He pulled over and stopped a couple of times, once at a lodge hall and once by some dumpsters where he climbed on his roof and hopped around while he appeared to tell himself a thing or three. He finally pulled onto the grounds of an abandoned plant or something. There were big brick buildings all overgrown with their windows busted out. I found a spot up the road to wait and watch and stuck with it until Jerry got peevish because the sun was setting and he had a bottle to buy.

He shut himself up in his room while I parked in a chair out on the landing and watched a man with a hairy back dog paddle across the pool. Soon enough I heard Jerry thumping around. It sounded from where I sat like he was yelling or weeping or something. Since we were trying to carry a woman back to Orlando to get licked, yelling and weeping seemed just the right thing to do.

ii

What even is sandalwood, and why would a man douse himself with it? Even one from Florida who saw fit to go around in puka shells?

Dottie's bird had come out of the wading pool and wandered over to where we were.

Viktor didn't seem to care about the gun in his ear. "Is this duck somebody's?" he asked me, "or is he just passing through?"

Russell came out of the house to see what I was up to. I'd started emptying Viktor's pockets onto the ground by then. A wallet, keys to a Pontiac, Listerine strips, some pennies and dimes, and a ziplock bag holding a couple of filthy rocks.

They were of special interest to Russell who mounted a disquisition.

"What's his trouble?" Viktor wanted to know as I pulled a pair of tin snips from his boot.

Once we'd tied him to a kitchen chair with about four feet of clothesline, he complained that we had trussed him up too tight.

"Got a shoulder thing." If he said it once, he said it a dozen times.

"What are you doing up here?" I asked him every way I could think to put it.

We were hindered by the fact that Viktor's first choice was to lie. Second and third and fourth choice too, so he laid out a bunch of nonsense about how him and Kelvin were neighbors and buddies who'd sworn to keep tabs on each other.

"Try again," I told him.

"He took money from me."

"What else?"

"Stole my girl."

"And you with all your technique."

He seemed to know what I meant. He winked.

Then he threw up a slew of other reasons why he'd come to Virginia. Nothing persuasive, just stuff he thought might work because Viktor's sort seems to think shooting you straight is pure dishonor, so he kept throwing up smoke and glancing (I noticed) at the stuff on the kitchen table. Most especially that baggie holding those filthy rocks.

So I picked it up. "What is this?"

Russell carried on at some length.

"Came in the lunchbox," Dottie said.

I could tell it wasn't gravel, but I've never been a gemstone kind of girl. "You here for these?" I asked Viktor.

Instead of lying, he went with, "Maybe." When I took a rock out for a closer look, Viktor shifted to, "Yeah."

"They're Uri's," he told me. "Going to need them back."

I got kind of a tingle, the sort I used to have as a detective when the nuggets of some whodunit started clicking into place.

"Were these Sue's?" is what I asked him.

"Skinny one with the Beamer?"

I nodded.

"Yeah, she gave them to us. I was just holding them for Uri, but that girl and the retard went and fouled that up."

I must not have looked sufficiently enlightened.

"Pinched them."

"Uri know?"

He shook his head. "I'm up here to head that off."

"What are they?"

"Emeralds or something. That's Uri's deal. Y'all give them back, I'm gone."

Russell didn't appear to like the sound of that and told us something about it at length. I looked to Dottie to translate for me, but she said instead, "Don't know."

"Let me try Jerry," I told them all, but my call went straight to voicemail. "What do y'all think?" I asked Russell and Dottie, which proved enough to send Russell straight over to the freezer where he pulled out a lump of foil. The item inside it was a frost-bitten human toe.

"Oh, right," I said and reminded Viktor he'd more or less killed a fellow.

"Never did."

Russell rattled off a lot of stuff, and I told Viktor, "He sure thinks so."

"Fellow had stuff going on," Viktor said. "Ticker maybe. I don't know."

That touched off more commentary from Russell and then a bit of talk from Dottie. "He's sure smelling up my kitchen," is all she said.

She had a point. Viktor's sandalwood stink was powerful and penetrating. I could taste a sour film of it on my teeth.

"Let's see what Jerry thinks," was my suggestion, and I recruited Russell and Dottie to help me drag Viktor out to the Chevy.

We left Viktor more or less upright on the back seat where he rode beside Russell and quizzed him for a while on his condition, but Russell didn't appear to approve of Viktor enough to blather at him. Instead, he made his noises Dottie's way, a few short, sharp spots of racket that Dottie didn't appear to have much trouble making out.

"He says," she told Viktor, "for you to shut on up."

It was a twenty-minute ride to our motel, and Viktor complained about his shoulder probably two-thirds of the way. For the balance he kept us posted that he couldn't feel his fingers. By the time I swung into the motel lot, Viktor was talking from the floorboard because we'd not bothered to belt him in, and I'd hit the brakes hard twice.

Jerry didn't make any noise when I knocked. That was uncommon for him. It had gotten to where he usually told me where exactly I ought to go and how damn quick I ought to pick up and go there. Then he'd generally burp or break some wind, but this time I got nothing back.

When I let myself in, I didn't see him at first, but I smelled him well enough.

Dottie came up behind me and said just, "Whew."

We found him down between the beds wearing just his underpants that he'd filled up instead of making his way to the toilet. He had leakage and crust and streaks here and there that looked like milk chocolate chiffon.

I didn't know what to do, or rather I knew what had to be done, but I didn't want to do it, so instead, I said, "Jesus," three or four times while staying pretty much where I was.

Dottie, for her part, merely told me, "Move."

I shifted enough to let her slip by me, and she grabbed Jerry by an ankle and dragged toward the bathroom. He grunted, uncorked some drunk English, and left kind of a trail on the rug.

I tried to make like I wanted to help, but I was queasy and disgusted, which Dottie immediately recognized well enough.

"I've got some practice," she told me and picked up speed once they'd hit the linoleum. She even tipped Jerry into the bathtub without getting anything on herself.

"He likes his rum," I chose to say by way of a general explanation.

"And his feed corn," Dottie added. She didn't appear to be bothered at all. "Every now and again," she said, "Russell'll really turn one loose."

So Dottie had experience and a process, which first involved a lot of water. She let the shower play on Jerry and even adjusted the temp enough so he wouldn't get scalded or chilled, which didn't keep him from complaining. Jerry shouted and thrashed around enough to come out of his socks. He worked his underpants down to around his knees, so Dottie squirted him strategically until she'd all but clogged the drain.

Along about then, I went outside. I said I was going to check on Viktor, but the truth is I'd seen all that I could stand.

I found Viktor in a complaining mood. His shoulder hurt. His fingers tingled. We'd left him on the back floorboard but he'd wriggled out into the lot and was roasting on a patch of sunny pavement. He'd attracted the attention of the motel manager's son who was always hanging around. He was probably five or six years old and wandered where he wanted, seemed to do pretty much whatever he pleased while his mother stayed in the office face-timing her friends and watching TV.

"What did he do?" the child wanted to know. His mother had named him Regis, and she'd been quick to volunteer it was for a friend of hers and not that TV guy.

Regis had a stick, and he was poking Viktor with it. Not with much force and just every now and again.

"Quit it," Viktor told him, but Regis giggled and carried on. "Hadn't got to be this way." That was directed at me. Viktor lifted his wrists so I could see that his hands were a bit on the pale side.

"Let's wait on Jerry. We'll figure something out."

"Quit it!"

Viktor kicked a leg out in Regis' direction and caught just enough of the child to knock him over.

The boy wailed at first and blubbered but then jabbed at Viktor in a frenzy.

Viktor told me to grab him, but I didn't. Regis tired out fairly quickly, and I did grab him once he started whacking our car.

Jerry and Dottie and Russell all came out fairly shortly thereafter, and Jerry looked about as well put together as I'd seen him in a while. His hair was combed. His shoes were tied. His shirt was tucked in all around, and I guess the whole experience of getting straightened out by Dottie had half sobered him up because he sounded fine.

"Uri send you?" Jerry asked Viktor without stopping off at Hello.

"I can't feel my arms."

Jerry nodded like he was sympathizing, but then he kicked

Viktor in a bicep. "How about now?"

Viktor moaned and rocked and made an attempt to invoke the Geneva Conventions though he couldn't recall what they were for or where exactly they'd come from.

"This is something about rocks?" Jerry asked Viktor. His Ss were a little loose and slobbery, but otherwise, he seemed fit to pass for straight.

Viktor went with, "Rummy," and Jerry kicked the other arm.

Russell pulled those gemstones from his pocket in their grimy ziplock bag and handed them over to Jerry.

Jerry held up the bag for study. Those rocks sure didn't look like much.

"Worth what?" Jerry asked.

"That's Uri's end," Viktor said. "I just hold stuff for him."

"And she took 'em? Naomi?"

"Guess so. Here they are."

That qualified for Jerry as lippy, so he kicked Viktor another time, appeared to catch him just below the ribcage."

Viktor tried to say something colorful but lacked the air to do it, so he sat and panted until he could manage, "Had them up at Lois' in a drawer."

"Dead lady in Tallahassee?" Jerry had a head for details even coming off a bender.

Viktor nodded. "Friend of mine." He got sad the way a chimpanzee might, by turning his lips inside out.

"Some kind of hooker wasn't she?" Jerry looked to be taking some pleasure.

"Singer," Viktor told him in a huff. "Made records. Was on the TV. Hung out with Frank and Dino and them."

"Your landlady, right?"

Viktor nodded. "Didn't need killing."

"Maybe you shouldn't have left stuff in her place that people might kill her over."

"That wasn't it," Viktor insisted.

"How can you know?" Jerry asked.

Viktor settled on "Wasn't," which he said in a pouty way three times, and then he volunteered, "I know where the girl is if you want her."

"I'd have maybe started off with that."

Viktor muttered another time, "Rummy."

Naturally, Jerry kicked him for it, and then Regis's mother called him in. She came far enough out of the motel office to tell her son, "Get over here."

He stayed where he was, of course, because he had a stick and people to poke.

"Y'all checking out, right?" she said to us. It didn't sound much like a question, but then Jerry's room smelled like a cow lot, so we were fine being told what to do.

"Take us to her," Jerry told Viktor.

He allowed he would on one condition. "Uri's rocks," he said. "I get them back."

"Fine," Jerry told him. "Let's get him up."

That job got left to me and Dottie, and together we hauled Viktor off the asphalt and shoved him into the car. He directed us clear across the county to a roller skating rink where we stopped in the lot, and we weren't alone there. Six or eight men were milling around and having what looked like a lively discussion.

"I kind of know these boys, some of them," Viktor told us as we pulled him out of the Chevy. "If they had any guts, I'd be drowned already."

One of those fellows recognized Viktor and pointed him out to the others.

"She told them I beat her and raped her and stuff." Viktor lip farted like that was absurd. "I mean, come on," he said my way mostly. "Look at me."

"She skate in there?" Jerry asked him.

Viktor shook his head and half pointed at the guys across the way. "She makes like she can tell their fortunes. They make like they're not staring at her tits."

BABYDOLL

i

He ran the store up the road where he sold gas sometimes but usually had sacks on his nozzles. Abernathy is what they called him, and most of his stuff was dusty and out of date. My mother didn't care what I told her about him because nobody but Abernathy would sell her Tareytons on time.

He smelled like Ben-Gay and Milk of Magnesia, and he'd make me stretch my panties out. When he'd seen enough, he'd pat me on the head and tell me, "Good."

You can't stay a regular kid for long when you're doing stuff like that. I wasn't equipped back then to understand what exactly he was up to, what I was up to, what we were up to together. I knew it wasn't regular business for him since most people just paid and left.

These days, as a grownup, I don't draw a lot of lines, and I'm convinced it all goes back to Abernathy.

I grew up in the barren DMZ between Florida and Georgia where everything was allowed but nothing much went on. We lived a few miles outside Metcalf, a half-hour from Tallahassee, so I went back and forth for a stretch between farmers and coked-up college boys and got even as a teen to the point where I could herd them like I wanted without causing suspicion for even a second that I was maybe in charge.

That's the trick of it, and it's hardly a chore since the job is to keep them believing what they believe already. If you take any kind of care, there's little chance a man will change his mind. Better still, I'd play along and let them have me like they wanted, and they'd usually get up to something they thought a desperado

might, but there was never anything genuinely rough or trouble-
some about them because most men are timid with women and
usually half ashamed of themselves.

None of them ever paid me outright. I didn't charge a rate. Instead, I made it easy for them to give me money if they wanted,
usually later in a way that could pass for something else.

They'd think they'd run across me or I'd happened onto them,
but I always laid my groundwork and did my research. So 'Doug'
was hardly an accident. Viktor before him wasn't either, and I
wouldn't have bothered with them if I'd not found Lois first.

She'd been a starlet way back, and I could see her house had
been a showplace. In her day, the woman had a fair few classy
boyfriends and a going singing career down in Miami. She was
known there as Lois Chevalier, but she was a Nevins from Hat-
tiesburg. She'd studied proper opera in Chicago, was on a TV
show or two, and then ended up singing torch songs at a night-
club on the miracle mile. She had a following because she could
hit a note and was a slinky girl.

Lois made a couple of records that not enough people bought
and hooked up for a while with a fellow who played a Nazi in a
movie where he got beat up by Frank Sinatra and shot by Ernest
Borgnine. She dropped the Nazi for a guy named Warren who
sold yachts and moved narcotics. He tried to marry her twice,
but she refused to have him either time. Then he drowned in
the straits with the help of some associates, and that's when Lois
decided Warren had been the man for her all along.

She went into showy mourning and drank more sloe gin than
was useful while actively resenting that Warren's assets had
been handed around to various people who weren't, conspicuously, her. So Lois was a woman with regrets and recriminations,
and I'd decided that, with a life like hers, she might have trinkets
as well. My idea was just to chat her up and get a look around her
place, and it seemed a boarder would be the easiest in for me.

Lois had six of them altogether. That'll tell you about the
size of her rambling house, and I didn't choose well initially but

started with a woman who lived downstairs in the back. I chatted her up in the CVS, and she let on she was buddies with Lois, but she proved to be a raving nut and soon got herself arrested while screaming something about sweet potatoes in a Bojangles parking lot.

So I shifted to Viktor. I'd noticed him coming and going, but he turned out to be a chore. He was dim and perfumy and pushed himself on me way too hard from the first. Worse still, there was something low and ethnic about the way he looked and sounded. He was authentically tight with Lois, though. That was clear enough.

Viktor made the mistake of confiding to me once that he hid stuff in her place. "Can't be too careful in this world," is what he chose to tell me. Then he said it again in gypsy or maybe Spanish or Greek like it was wisdom from way over there instead of just ordinary.

I might even have stuck with Viktor if he'd not put me onto Doug, who Viktor called, "the retard down the hall."

Doug was big and quiet and had a dent in his head. He didn't look like a guy who could bring himself to bother a girl for sex, and it had gotten to where that was about all Viktor wanted. To his credit, Viktor wasn't nearly as bad at it as most men can be, but he stayed way too proud of the maneuvers he got up to. Soon enough I got worn out with pretending he was truly setting me off, so I shifted to 'Doug' who wasn't retarded, wasn't even in fact 'Doug'.

Kelvin Fergus Mackie was his given name, and he'd been in the bughouse for a stretch after a blow-up with some neighbor girl and his family that had ended with felony charges and a fair few broken bones.

'Doug' didn't take much cultivating, and he put me with Lois right away, but our visit went more poorly than I'd hoped. She turned out to be a tedious hag. Lois was bitter, and she was petty, and once she'd finished with all the nasty things she could say about folks she'd known, she sized me up and fired a few barbs my way.

I'll allow I tapped her a touch too hard, but that was more in disappointment than anger. I hit her with an ashtray I'd been admiring, a fine piece of leaded crystal with quite a lot of heft.

I didn't tell 'Doug' what to think. He could see the lump for himself along with the stuff I'd piled on the coffee table. So I left him to do what he wanted and only nudged him after a while. It hardly took much to get 'Doug' to join me on the bus up to Atlanta. Nuthouse aside, I was fairly eager to have a large man around.

'Doug' might not have been instructable, but I could aim him well enough. Percy found that out and served to balance the ledger. While Lois might have been on me, Cousin Percy was chiefly on him, and sometimes you need cement like that to make for better partners. It didn't hurt that it turned out I even liked 'Doug' well enough. He had no blather to him and would as soon just sit and stare out the window as have any sort of manly leer in my direction. Sure he had his antsy episodes, real nuthouse residue, but he'd usually feel them coming on and take them out and away.

I remember 'Doug' talking one day about how, when he was in the bughouse, they'd sometimes tie him to a board and carry him outside, leave him laid out on a couple of sawbucks.

"It was all right," 'Doug' told me. "Sunshine and all." Occasionally he'd even get company, some other nut tied to a board as well.

'Doug' said it was often a fellow named Carter who'd ended up at Hotchkiss after killing a regular pile of people. Nobody he knew, just people he'd see and decide somehow he fancied. That was Carter's word for it, 'Doug' told me, and fancying was a mysterious thing.

I can't say I do plans and strategies, not ordinarily and as a rule. I know people think I'm conniving and devious in an organized way, but I'm usually just shifting off of one thing and heading for another, which probably looks more thought out than it feels. A day doesn't pass when I'm not testing and gauging the options before me. Byron, for instance. I had to think some legitimate child would come along to take my place, but until then I hoped being scarce and flirty would work on Byron a little. Sometimes the farther away you wander, the more powerful your pull.

Chiefly, I was killing time with 'Doug', and he was good to have for a backstop because you can never quite know when some stray man might try to lay on hands, and Doug functioned as six and a half feet of I-don't-think-so. He did it for me at the skating rink and most days he did it back home where the guy who owned the house we rented made a point of coming over to direct a lot of piffle my way. He probably would have been handsy but for 'Doug' merely hanging around.

We were content enough as colleagues and associates, me and 'Doug', particularly once we settled into our little farmhouse in the country with its busted asbestos shingles and its furnace in the floor. Our landlord kept cattle, three muddy heifers that bellowed whenever they saw him, and they all passed most of each day just standing and rubbing against the fence.

The guy's name was Ruben, and his wife had left him ten or twelve years before. He told us she'd run off with the fuel-oil man and said he'd never missed her much. I read Ruben's palm one afternoon for no particular reason, had him sit at our little breakfast table where I made up a bunch of nonsense about some money in a can buried out in his side yard that he needed to find before a dog or something got to it.

"Ain't no dogs around here," he told me.

I ran a finger along his palm, and that had the effect of shutting Ruben right up.

I got the idea from our neighbor Cheryl back at the trailer park, who couldn't decide if she wanted to be a stripper or a fortune teller and was almost certain to fail at either one because failing at stuff was kind of what Cheryl did. I, however, could sell it because I have a gift for prattle and I'm not afraid to show off my 34 Ds.

The first place we tried the act out was the spot where we stayed and stuck. It was ten minutes up the road at the grill by the skating rink. Men mostly congregated there to wait for their wives and their kids. I'd bought three feet of velour in a fabric shop, and that first night I spread it on a table, lit a big, spice-scented candle, and then meditated for a bit. I had a jar with folding money in it that I set across the way so as to suggest it didn't matter to me if I got compensated. I knew the men, of course, would fight to fill it. That's kind of what men do.

'Doug' planted himself against the wall, and it was a comfort to know he was handy in case I ran into some trouble I couldn't work clear of by myself.

It all played out well enough. After maybe a week, we had a regular flock of patrons who'd ask me questions about their prospects while I cradled one of their hands in both of mine. As a rule, I'd wear some low cut thing, and those boys would give me shifty ganders, but then they'd always shove some money in my jar.

'Doug' only had to tangle with a couple of spirited guys from a motorcycle crew, but he was more than large and capable enough to manage. Lots of men believe they're fighters and get involved in the sort of scraps where fellows shove each other around and come up maybe a little bloody, but 'Doug' wasn't the sort to tussle in a recreational way. He'd locate your tender plac-es and make you suffer. If a couple of your joints got knocked apart and a bone or two got splintered, that was the price of mix-ing it up with a Hotchkiss alum.

We were all right, then, me and 'Doug'. Off hours, we'd do separate stuff. It got to where 'Doug' was frequently out riding around in the car while I was trying my best to keep life bumpy for Byron. A man can forget he needs to lick you if you don't remind him every day.

Then I looked up one evening from my patch of velour and there was Viktor from Tallahassee. Since I don't believe in coincidences, I knew he was trouble straightaway. He tried to hang back and keep out of sight, but the stink of Viktor reached me, so I sensed he was there before I'd even managed to scope him good.

He winked once he knew I'd seen him. He looked for all the world like a man who was pleased he'd come so far to be where he was, and I tried to work an inventory in my head of all of Lois' goods. From what I could remember, none of it screamed Viktor to me. In fact, it had mostly turned out to be pretty indifferent junk.

The reasonable approach would have been for me to ask Viktor what he wanted, but since 'Doug' at that moment was off somewhere having one of his itchy fits, I was on my own with my deck of cards, my money jar, and my square of velour along, of course, with some of my usual clientele. I decided to put those boys to work and so whimpered and pointed Viktor's way while I gave them a yarn that ended up with rape.

Viktor laughed. I blubbered (I can turn on the waterworks), so a few of those fellows closed on Viktor and proceeded to wrap him up.

I knew if Viktor could find me, I was hardly scarce enough, and since 'Doug' wasn't handy to pick me up, I asked Kenny, one of my regulars, if I could have brief use of his car. I made it sound like I needed some lady product as a consequence of seeing Viktor, and Kenny wasn't going to quiz me on it but just handed over his keys.

He drove a powder-blue Fairlane he must have Simonized twice a week, and while Kenny hardly seemed the sort who much liked people touching his stuff, I'd traced his lifeline plenty of times and knew he was weak against my cleavage, so I gave him a peck on the cheek like he might get a favor back. I'd long since learned that men are ever hopeful.

I swung by the house to grab some stuff and then headed for the interstate in Kenny's shiny car. I stopped at the Sheetz to top her up, and a man (of course) came over. He had on some kind of uniform like he was maybe half a cop.

"Kenny's isn't it?" he wanted to know.

I made like I couldn't quite hear him.

"Can't say I've ever known him to lend her out."

I told him we ought to call Kenny up and said I'd dropped my phone on the floorboard. Once he'd gone in snout first after it, I started hitting him with a wrench. It wasn't as big a wrench as I would have wanted, had been stuck under the driver's seat, so I had to drum on him for a while.

Finally, he quit moving once he'd told me something like, "Nrrggrrff."

ii

According to his ID, the fellow's name was Norman and he worked for some sort of security biz that probably rattled doorknobs and such. I carried him up the road a bit and pulled off into an abandoned fun park. The place had carpet golf links with a go-kart track beside it, and the whole business was surrounded by rickety, weathered Civil War dioramas, chiefly scenes of battle painted on puckered plywood. Cold Harbor. Bull Run. Brandywine Station. Like that.

The art was grade-school level. The horses all looked like sheep with saddles. Most of the soldiers' hands were bigger than their heads, and all of the bluecoats had pointy goatees like they'd just boiled up out of hell.

The whole place was weedy and trash-strewn, and every wooden thing in the vicinity was, at very best, half-rotten. That included the cutout of General Lee by the entrance to the Putt-Putt, which featured a dilapidated windmill and a plasterwork camel that was lath wood and chicken wire from about its four knees down.

I took a walking tour of the entire park, from First Bull Run to Appomattox before I went back to the car to see if Norman was still holding on. He came off as dead-ish, a little cold to the touch, and he looked to have about a pint of blood in his hair, but he moaned and grunted as I tugged and wrangled to get him out of the car.

I took pains to suggest to Norman that what Kenny did with his Fairlane ought to be pretty much up to Kenny alone, and since Norman was far too heavy to drag, I poked him until he crawled. We eventually reached a walkway that was weedy cinders underfoot with collapsed rail fencing on either side. Norman made it under his own steam to Spotsylvania Courthouse before he lost all headway and piled up in a heap.

I decided to give him a quarter-hour or so to just expire, and I tapped him with a chunk of fencing in a bid to help him along since driving off and leaving a man half dead seemed shiftless to me. I passed the time taking in the dioramas, and aside from the names of the battles and the odd bridge or church or ridgeline, they all came off as pretty much the same. Canon balls exploding. Bloody limbs flying through the air. That and sheep with saddles and men with hands like dinner plates.

I kept circling back to find Norman still lingering and hanging on. Of course, the easy thing would have been to tap the man a few times further, but homicide isn't really one of my things. Manslaughter, however, is usually within reach, so I thought about running him over with Kenny's car. I held off, though, and gave him another fifteen minutes because he was looking pale and puny, and I worked to improve my time by making proper plans.

I had to think I'd need to ditch Kenny's car since it had become kind of a crime scene, so I figured I'd keep to backroads all the way down to Lynchburg where I'd catch a bus or maybe take the train, just about anything on offer heading south.

If Byron needed more time and tinkering, I could hang somewhere down there, I'd known luck on the gulf before with a lawyer from Perdido who did me the service of having a coronary and two fully estranged sons.

I was still turning all my options over in my head when an SUV came off the road, a black one, new and shiny, hardly the sort the locals drove. It stopped right beside the Fairlane, and once the driver had rolled out, I took a walk in his direction to try to keep him clear of Norman. I knew right away I'd seen the guy before. He'd been sitting at the bar in the skating rink grill while those boys took care of Viktor. I remembered him because he was big and boxy and dressed in a shiny suit that couldn't seem to decide if it was blue or gray.

His head was shaved and shiny too, and one of his ears looked half chewed off. He didn't fit in with the dioramas any more than he had at the rink.

He smiled and said something my way. He was coming easy, strolling. He ignored all the rubbishy stuff out there but instead stayed fixed on me.

"What do you need?" I asked him.

He just kept on strolling and grabbed me by the elbow before I could slip away.

"You come, *kukla*," is what he told me. He clearly wasn't local, and I guessed I could go with the arm he was holding or stay behind without it. So I let him steer me and nearly had to trot just to keep up. We stopped alongside that black SUV at the door behind the driver's. It opened, and a gentleman stepped out.

I'd seen plenty of men like him before. Polo shirt. Madras trousers. Bridle loafers. Socks at home. He favored me with the brand of smile I'd tolerated more than my share of. When he finally spoke he told me, "Hey here, *shefela*."

I was trying to work out what I ought to do and how maybe I ought to do it when chewed ear poked me and indicated I needed to answer back. Him I told, "Keep your hair on." Bridle loafers just got, "Hey."

I probably should have known who he was. I'd spent a lifetime hearing about him, but he wasn't the type of guy to let his picture get around. We'd all heard stories of things he'd done and had run across people he'd done them to. A girl I knew had a brother who worked with a fellow they called Stumpy who'd gotten behind on an obligation back in the machete days. Stumpy had ended up losing most of his left hand.

If he'd been worthless ten years later, it might have only cost him a toe. This life, like almost everything, is pretty much all in the timing.

So while I eventually figured out who I was dealing with, there at first it was just a musclehead with a chewed-up ear and a man who looked like he ought to be sipping Mount Gay at the clubhouse grill.

"Please," Mount Gay told me and made it clear I needed to climb in his SUV. Chewed ear helped me along, of course. He pretty well tossed me in. There was nothing to give the game away, just two copies of *Kiplinger's*, an empty corn chip bag, and a yellow travel cup from South of the Border.

Chewed ear climbed in behind the wheel, but he just sat, and we stayed where we were.

"Who's your friend, bubbula?" Mount Gay asked me as he pointed at nothing much.

"What friend?"

Chewed ear pulled out a phone and got a video going. He handed it over the seatback, and I found myself looking at me. Me talking to Norman at the Sheetz. Me tapping Norman with a wrench. Me tucking him fully into the Fairlane. Me looking around and heading off.

"Got handsy. End of my rope with that stuff."

That earned me a snort from Mount Gay who said a thing to chewed ear in whatever language *shefala/bubbula* was. Then chewed ear reached around and smacked me, caught me right across the ear. I believe he used an open hand, though with his sort it hardly mattered since you got a couple of pounds of swinging beef either way.

It was one of those sharp, professional blows. I saw the aurora borealis and tasted gutter nails.

By the time I could focus again, Mount Gay was humming a tune to himself and busy plucking fuzz off his pants.

"Car there belongs to some buddy of his. I borrowed it for more than I said." I'd been around men long enough to know they'll keep on pounding, so you might as well give them whatever they want as soon as you reasonably can.

"Where you headed?" Mount Gay asked me. He was fooling with his cuticles by then.

"Thinking up north, like Scranton or somewhere."

"All your stuff in there?" He glanced at Kenny's Fairlane.

I nodded. "Trunk. Key's in it."

Chewed ear rolled out of the SUV and unlocked the Fairlane trunk lid. He fished out my stuff and spread it across the lot. What I hadn't thrown in loose I'd only shoved in grocery sacks, and he dumped it all out onto the ground and moved it around with his foot.

"If you tell me what you're after, we might can straighten all this out."

"*Bay nakht zenen ale ki shvartz*," Mount Gay told me, or something sort of like it. Then he swung his door open and translated for me. "At night, *shefala*, all cows are black."

Mount Gay didn't jerk me when he took my arm. He was the sort who clearly thought himself too civilized for that. He just dragged me out behind him with one relentless, steady pull.

Once we'd come around to the Fairlane, chewed ear told Mount Gay, "*Nichego.*"

"Where are they?" Mount Gay asked me.

I didn't know what they wanted and was resigning myself to shortly ending up bloody on the ground.

"I believe we have a mutual friend," he said. Then he told me like a Russian count might (or one from Transylvania), "Viktor."

"Oh." I didn't say it so much as have it just leak out. I suddenly knew exactly who he was. "Uri, right?"

He bowed.

I don't mind saying I felt queasy. Yes, he'd gone from machete to snips and was said to have mellowed a bit, but I'd heard about him taking off a man's head with a shovel.

"Yeah, I know Viktor a little. We went out. It didn't last."

Uri said something foreign back and then told me what it was, one of those love-as-a-fading-flower sorts of things. Aside from the active threat of losing digits, Uri was seeming a bore.

"His friend," he said. "Singer," he told me. "The dead one."

"Lois?"

He nodded. Then he asked me, "You?"

"Me what?"

Somehow without even getting the slightest of glance from his boss, chewed ear knew to smack me in the head. His fist might have been closed for this one because he drove me onto the ground.

"What do you want?" I asked Uri. "I mean...exactly?"

That earned me a snorty laugh. Then Uri told me something else in *shefala/bubala*, and I got smacked again. Open hand this time and something close to gently. The sky only went briefly purple. I tasted a penny in my mouth.

"'Doug's' got it, whatever it is," I said. "He hit her with an ashtray. I helped him clean her out. Probably shouldn't have, looking back." I do remorse like a pro.

Uri gave me a hand up off the ground. "Gemstones," he said. "Would have looked like rocks to you."

I remembered them, of course. Two rocks in a baggie, and I'd only brought them along because they were in with some other stuff. I'd put them off as something I'd try to make sense of later. Now there was Uri making sense of them for me and coming all the way up from the gold coast, which laid a price on them as well.

I went dumb, of course. It seemed the safest route. I told him I remembered a couple of rings and two or three ladies' watches.

He didn't have to describe those rocks to me because chewed ear had a picture of them on his phone. They were laid out side by side on what looked like a hand towel with a folded dollar bill next to them for scale.

"We have a motivated buyer," Uri told me, "but no stones. You see the problem?"

"Doug'll know."

"What do you suggest?" Uri asked me.

"I guess we go find him."

"And this one?" He had a look beyond me to where I figured Norman was.

"Leave him," was my take. "He'll either be all right or he

won't."

Uri made out to be amused. "Handsy," is all he said.

Then chewed ear punched me in the stomach, threw me over his shoulder, and pitched me onto the backseat of their car. It was proving a lively thing to be the object of Uri's attention. I rode right next to Uri who gave me his handkerchief to blot at a scrape on my hand and then had chewed ear stop at the Outback hard by the interstate where he went in and ate a ribeye while we waited in the car.

After that, we pulled in at a motor lodge because Uri wasn't, he told me, the sort to chase around after folks in a reckless way.

"It'll all keep," he said. He seemed a long way from machetes or using a shovel to relieve some some guy of his head.

They took two rooms. I got to stay in the one with chewed ear and about half expected to pass my night there getting brutalized, but he taped me up and left me alone. Out of the car and away from Uri, chewed ear came off seeming just big and boxy and sad.

We only got rolling again late morning after Uri had conducted a spot of pressing business on the phone. Then it was back to normal, and chewed ear pitched me onto the backseat again. I steered them in the direction of Del-Jo-Ray acres, meant to guide them to our blue trailer where I hoped they'd let their guard down just enough so I could bolt.

We were a good half hour reaching the place, and Uri thumbed through a *Kiplinger's* on the way. He troubled himself to give me a spot of investment advice, or I think that's what he meant anyway when he said to me, "Kombucha." Then he asked me to explain to him why tattoos were all the rage.

"Don't know," I told him. "Don't have any." I figured if they found my skylark things would already be pretty well over for me.

Once we'd turned into Del-Jo-Ray acres and Uri had had a look around, the only thing he could think to say was, "*Oy.*"

"Kelvin picked it," I said. "I couldn't get away from him. He's big, you know?"

"Oh *shefela*," Uri said back. He wasn't being sympathetic. I got the distinct sense he'd counted on me lying better than I was.

"That one," I told chewed ear, and he stopped in front of our blue trailer. "Closet in the bedroom. Ought to be a bank bag and a couple of boxes in there."

We all got out of the SUV, but only chewed ear went inside, and right on cue bike boy rode over to see what was up. Sometimes people are dead reliable *because* of their shiftlessness.

"Hey," he said, primarily to my chest.

"Come for some stuff," I told him. Just then chewed ear stepped out to show us the busted flip flop he'd found on the closet shelf.

"Where'd it go?" I asked bike boy.

He told my sternum, "What?"

I described the bank bag and the boxes and said I knew he'd carted them off. Because he was such a chiseler, he couldn't be sure he hadn't done it right up until Uri took enough of an interest to draw out his pair of snips.

"Man," bike boy said, "those are nice."

"Her things?" Uri asked the boy.

"All kinds of people been through here."

"Oh?"

"Door ain't even shut. Had a duck in and out of there for a while."

Chewed ear just needed a glance from Uri to take firm hold of bike boy who told him, "Hey!" and "Quit it!" and that sort of stuff, which was when I started to back up and announced I'd soon be peeing. Once I'd put a bush between me and them, I took off at a trot.

Only bike boy yelled for me to come back. Uri and chewed ear didn't seem to much care, so I kept on hoofing it and made decent headway even in my girly shoes.

I headed out across what had been a pond, but the water had all dried up, and the sun had about half cooked the ground, so it was crusty in large patches but still a little sloppy here and there. On the far side was a paved road, and that's where I was aiming. I could see traffic on it up and down. I planned on looking distressed enough to snag a ride with some man and persuade him to take me farther than he'd likely meant to go.

Climbing up the bank on the far side wasn't an easy matter, and I'm sure I was kind of a sight by the time I reached the road, but lucky for me, the first guy along had cataracts and shouldn't have been driving. He'd told me as much once I'd climbed in his truck and convinced him I was a girl.

"Y'all ought not to be out here," he said. "No telling who'll come along."

His name was Mercer, and I got to hear about his dead wife and his dog that sometimes barked at clouds when it wasn't digging holes in his yard.

"I had a good dog once," he told me, "but this ain't him."

I said I was hoping to get to Lynchburg. Mercer recalled he'd bought some tires there once.

He drove awfully slowly, and I would have hurried him along, but he was all over the road going thirty, so I left him to creep as he pleased. We'd gone maybe three or four miles when chewed ear went roaring past us and swooped into our lane. He stopped too quick, and Mercer hit him. Tapped him anyway, and then chewed ear climbed out and came stalking back to bounce Mercer's head off his steering wheel.

Chewed ear crooked a finger my way, didn't even bother to say, "Come."

Bike boy was sitting on the backseat where I'd sat before. The t-shirt he'd been wearing around his neck like he usually wore them was being used to dab at an oozing wound where a nipple had been.

"We seem to have come up empty on those boxes," is what Uri chose to go with.

Bike boy informed my sternum, "Don't like you much right now."

I guess they figured they'd drained bike boy of all his use-
fulness because chewed ear snatched him up and pitched him
straight into the road.

RUMMY

The truth is I felt sorry for her and not even because of the hair. A buddy had heard I was scouting around and threw her into the mix because he knew a guy who knew a guy who thought she was all right. I needed a woman to see after female clients in places and ways I couldn't and, haircut aside, she qualified for that.

I came to like her well enough. The girl had made a mistake. She'd shot a civilian who'd not (at that moment) needed to be shot. I had a fair idea of what that felt like. I'd run over a guy with my cruiser but was able to lie about it because he never woke up again. I'd swing by to see him from time to time in the place where his family put him and make like I was struggling with remorse. Occasionally I'd even sit and pray with his sister and his mother. They'd come to believe he'd dashed into the road because he was gloomy and low.

I don't know about that. I seem to recall he was crossing with the light, but I had two pints in me and so can't really be sure.

I went to meetings after and even quit cold for a while, but you've got to have something to stick in the hollow once you've set the bottle aside. Me and the missus had long since busted up, our daughter was God knows where, and my spaniel just laid on the throw rug groaning and making fatty tumors. I bought a bicycle and rode it for nearly a week, but both of my knees objected, so I took up walking, which eventually put me in front of the liquor store. I quit again about four months later once they'd retired me off the job, and I stayed sufficiently quasi-sober to land some work as a consultant. In my case, that meant I had to be up for just about any damn thing.

I'd worked sex crimes for nearly a decade and had a feel for skeevy people, which probably explains how we ended up with a client list of kinkers. Not any outright evil ones but just the sort with wayward itches and microscopic self-restraint. Chiefly we paid off loose ends and cauterized indiscretions because our clients were intent on passing for respectable even though they conspicuously weren't. We'd advise on best behaviors, but nobody ever listened, so we chiefly worked as glorified bagmen instead. If my partner had qualms, she kept them to herself.

I'd debated about taking on Byron from Orlando because he had a thing for minors, and usually even piles of money won't help you get away with that. Byron, though, didn't want actual sex. He licked the inside of elbow joints and the backs of knees, and he was so brief and precise about it that it could come off seeming harmless, just odd and a little eccentric and passingly disgusting as well. Then he'd toddle off to pleasure himself and come back grinning and smelling of Germ-X.

I'm not sure how I would have felt if Byron had a go at my child. Or rather, I am sure how I would have felt but chose not to think about it because Byron always overpaid us and did it with inches of cash. We had nothing to do with the girls who hung around his pool. Instead, we tamped down collateral upset and smoothed over knobby patches until Byron, to my considerable shock, fell in something like love.

Naomi Fay Runyon from Metcalf, Georgia, and she seemed a surprising choice because she wasn't as young or as pretty as most of the girls in Byron's harem. She was twenty-seven, we'd come to find out, but she dressed like she was twelve, and she had such a vinegary disposition that whenever Byron licked her, you'd have thought the girl was having a molar pulled.

Clearly, she was playing Byron. My partner and I agreed on that, and we had to believe this Naomi was after a genuine chunk of money. But Byron had plenty and was free to do with it whatever he pleased. We just wanted to make sure he had all the available details on her first, so my partner trailed Naomi and gathered up a damning assortment. When Byron reviewed them and mentioned a few of them to her, she had a snit and left the state.

That's when he decided he loved the girl and had to have her back. He wasn't open to hearing sense after that but instead gave us one of his Biscayne sedans and an envelope of cash. Pretty much all he told us was, "Don't come back without her."

Naomi left such a gaudy trail we could hardly help but track her down. We were all but homing in on her when a guy named Viktor came rolling up as well. I immediately knew that meant that Uri, his boss, had an interest in her too.

I'll admit I'd been indulging myself before Viktor came around. It had gotten to where I'd leave my partner to go out and do the grunt work while I stayed back at whatever motel we were in and got fully sloshed in daylight. The only theory I have to explain it is that I'd lost interest in everything. I didn't care if Byron hooked up with Naomi and she plundered him down to the fittings, so it hardly mattered to me if we found her tomorrow or next week. Either way, we'd have to convince her to ride back to Florida with us, which meant she'd need first to strike some deal with Byron sufficient to draw her home.

Because I wasn't so keen on what had to be done, I stayed back at the motel and drank. But then Viktor showed up, or rather my partner found him and brought him around, and that happened to be the day I hit the bottom of the ditch.

My partner had been letting me do my worst and not saying much about it. She'd knock on my door most mornings. "Guess I'm going," she'd usually tell me and then leave me a gap to answer, but I don't think I ever did. When she'd get back in the afternoons, she'd usually pop in for a look, but she never tried to steer me off the bottle.

She had teamed up with a local rent-a-cop. I was aware of that, had even seen the woman once back when I was still half sober, but I didn't know anything about her except that she was fat and old. Then we met, me and her, under unsavory circumstances.

She was upright and presentable while I was on the floor covered in crap. My partner had come in, her rent-a-cop too, and some man I didn't know who made remarks in what sounded like German. I remember thinking I was hardly the sort of thing he'd probably come stateside to see.

I was in and out of focus there on the floor, which is probably the best way to be when you're rum paralyzed and your bowels have let go. So I can't say I was truly aware of what was going on until I felt myself being dragged across the carpet by one leg. I tried to protest and complain but just crapped some more instead, and the next thing I knew I'd been dumped in the tub, and the water was pouring down on me.

I'm not the kind of drunk who apologizes. There are plenty of those around. They get equal parts wasted and pathetic, usually whine and moan and blubber. I'm more the prickly sort with no use much for remorse. We do what we do and we are what we are, and there's really no point in doing a thing but shutting up about it. So I didn't say I wished I wasn't a drunk who's shat himself all over, but instead I complained rent-a-cop had hosed me down while I was still in my shirt and briefs.

She pulled my clothes off of me eventually, and I'll allow that I was revolting. So I got sluiced, and I got scrubbed, and then got made to rinse myself while rent-a-cop brewed up a tiny pot of bitter motel room coffee, which I ended up drinking most of straight from the spout.

I've got a history of getting drunk slowly but sobering up at double speed, and that's kind of what happened. The diarrhea probably flushed me out a little, and then the shower cleared my head enough so I could speak.

I remember pointing and asking her, "Who's he?"

"Russell," she said.

That didn't help much.

Then rent-a-cop told me, "My mister."

Russell wasn't about to be left out and added quite a lot of something himself.

By then, I was probably as straight as I'd been for the better part of a week, and rent-a-cop and her mister retired once I'd asked for privacy to get decent. I was aware that somebody, my partner I guessed, had mentioned lowlife Viktor by name. That's why my thoughts couldn't help but stray for a while in Uri's general direction.

I had history with Uri. I'd more or less known him since back when he was muscle for a Cuban, a job Uri hardly looked suited for because he was scrawny and sort of a runt and so couldn't just go out and bust up guys the way his associates did. Most of those boys were piles of meat who got on through brute force and leverage. Uri recognized he'd have to make his mark some other way, and he'd soon found his niche with ruthlessness.

It was a practical business decision Uri made because he was ambitious. I never got the feeling he was bent or evil. Uri simply recognized he had to go at folks in an alarming way, and that's where the machete came in. Blood and butchery never much bothered Uri. He was profoundly unsentimental, so he could threaten to take a couple of toes from some delinquent customer and then pull out his blade and actually do it without having to work up the nerve.

Uri had tried weight lifting and had spent a few months getting stretched at a chiropractor's office, but it turned out a machete and the will to use it was all that he required.

We picked him up after a clerical error. I was still in uniform back then, and Uri had gone to the wrong address and hacked off bits of the wrong householder because his Cuban boss or one of his minions had transposed a seven and a three, which meant the man who should have been short some digits saw the trouble from up the block and put in a call to the PD about some nut with a machete.

It didn't help him much. He got tenderized a week or so later by one of Uri's colleagues who had the proper number and showed up with his fists.

Uri was upset by the time we reached him. He was not the

type who could tolerate mistakes with any grace, and he'd only become aware he was in the wrong house a couple of fingers in when he compared notes with the man he was working on, who claimed to be a dentist, and not the kind of dentist who'd be into Cubans for nearly thirty grand. His house was nice. The man had toy poodles and Jesusy decor all over the place.

That didn't mean he couldn't have a drug or maybe a gambling problem, but the guy felt off to Uri, so Uri was on the horn with his Cubans when we came into the house. He sounded to be trying and failing to translate *fuckwit* into Spanish.

We located Uri out in that dentist's detached garage where he'd bandaged up the fellow's bloody hand. He pointed out the machete before offering up his wrists and saying, "Isn't this a righteous mess?"

That was Uri's first and only arrest, and his Cuban got to the dentist somehow who ended up insisting the amputations had been accidental. He said he was clumsy with machetes and had grabbed Uri's by the blade. So the case eventually fell apart, but while we were booking Uri, I spent a couple of hours with him, and he proved to be a chatty rascal. He let me know he was no common thug but an authentic entrepreneur who'd tied into his Cuban out of convenience but wouldn't require him for long.

It was just me and him sitting there at a desk while I typed up his paper, and I guess because he could deny it later, he told me all grades of stuff. Uri said he'd known a psychotic back when he was just a boy and remembered how he'd acted, told me he'd decided that lunacy worked to exceedingly useful effect.

"It pays to be a man," is what he said, "who'll do about any damn thing."

We'd bagged his bloody machete and laid it on a table, and that's along about when I glanced at the thing and told him, "No style to that."

I've got to hand it to Uri. Even back then when he was young and raw and cocky, he wasn't the sort to be defensive as well. He heard people out, even the ones he'd shown up just to lay open and hack on. He didn't say much else to me. I finished his forms and routed him through. He was sprung on bail in only a couple of hours and never even went to trial. I didn't see Uri again for some years, but I certainly heard about him, most particularly that he was still lopping digits but had graduated to snips.

They were Stanley tin snips to be precise that he sharpened with a stone. Word was those snips had the sort of edge you could slice through rebar with.

I say all that to say just this: I felt at least partly to blame. No man with a machete is likely to get ahead for long, but a man like Uri – with snips in his pocket – could create an illusion. A machete lets you out of that. You might as well be missing teeth.

So I happened across him young and rough and then saw him again at Sue's. It was something like thirty years later, and he was established and refined. Uri's trousers were linen. He was far too swanky to bother with socks. He had a two-hundred-dollar haircut and lacquer on his nails.

Viktor at the time was still enchanting Sue with his remarkable technique, and he let on Uri was just some pal he'd brought around for laughs. So they all had a drink and a chat and then Sue led Uri on a tour of her house. Since she was not the sort to much care about her stuff, Uri sized it all up and cared about it for her.

"Where'd y'all find him?" I'd put on clean trousers and stepped out into the motel parking lot by then.

Rent-a-cop and the German looked at me like I must have been body-snatched, but my partner had seen me recover before at warp speed from rummy stupors.

"Appreciate it," I said to rent-a-cop like maybe she'd lent me a dollar instead of dragged me into a motel bathroom and cleaned up my nasty self.

I got "Right" back, which was about what I deserved.

"Show him," my partner said to rent-a-cop's mister, and he pulled a baggie out of his pocket and shook two rocks in my face.

"Jewels of some kind," my partner told me. "Sue's weren't

they?"

I nodded. "How'd they get up here?"

That set off rent-a-cop's mister who weighed in for a while. While it was impossible to tell just what he was saying, he proved to be adamant about it and repeated for emphasis a couple of points that he was keen to make.

Rent-a-cop told me, "I don't know," even before I could ask her to translate.

"What does Viktor have to say about it?" I wanted to know.

My partner pointed at our Chevy. "Go ask him."

The manager's kid was over by Viktor poking stuff with a stick. Viktor was sitting on the asphalt with his wrists zip-tied together.

Once he saw me coming, Viktor spat at the child and then said, "Do something with him."

I did shift the boy aside but only after I'd let him poke Viktor in several of his tender places.

Skating rinks all smell the same. It's probably feet and floor wax, but Naomi Fay Runyon had been working a nice one as far as countryside roller rinks go. I went in on my own for a scour while Viktor tangled with some buddies in the lot. They were under the distinct impression he'd forced himself on Naomi, but Viktor insisted he was far too dashing to ever have to chase a woman down. That fared poorly with those boys in the lot because they had eyes and they had noses.

The guy tending bar in the rink grill didn't want to tell me anything straightaway.

"Don't think I'm supposed to," is about all I could get from him. It turned out he'd watched a lot of TV shows where bartenders were greedy with details.

I showed him the badge I carry for putting in front of people like him, and I said I had reason to think Naomi had witnessed a homicide and an assault.

"That's why she's up here," I told him. "Hiding out, you know?"

"She in trouble?"

"Not from us. Just want to hear what she saw."

He told me, "Hmm," and poured me a coffee since I was on duty and all. I probably would have asked for a jolt to go with it, but they had just beer and lousy wine. That helped put my alchy itches down.

The bartender looked in both directions like he was about to cross a freeway. There wasn't anybody near us, just some farmer type on his phone who sounded like he was selling soybeans or buying laying hens. He kept saying stuff on the order of, "Naw, thirty-two, and we'll double up." Then he'd listen for a bit and go with something like, "And can't none of them be culls."

The bartender eventually caught his eye and then twitched his head in such a way as to drive that fellow over toward the rink. Only then did he lean in and tell me, "She was here. Took Kenny's Ford."

"Stole it?"

He snorted. "Kind of made him give it to her."

"They an item?"

"Don't he wish."

"Made him give it to her how?"

"You seen her?"

"Not lately."

He cupped his hands to give himself a pair of double ds.

"Chesty seems to count for an awful lot around here."

He gawked at me like he wondered what galaxy I'd swooped in from. He told me the customers made a point of stuffing money in her jar because they were fond of her and wanted to keep her solvent and safe. He said it like it was a brotherly thing and had nothing to do with her curves.

"Been gone since yesterday," he told me.

"She say where?"

He shook his head.

"Kenny know?"

He couldn't be sure he didn't.

"Which one's he?" I asked him.

"The one that looks like he might cry."

Viktor was getting roughed up again. He had a knack of coming across as if he was in need of a smack. There are men all over who impress other men that way. You don't have to know them or even hear from them, just one glance and you're making a fist.

That scrum of boys in the lot had effectively closed him off and swallowed him up. They looked to be tussling with Viktor, the way men often will. Lots of threats and nudges and shoves, which couldn't have been pleasant for him. I caught snatches of his sales job as he tried to explain to those boys how everything they thought they knew was wrong. Those fellows were egging each other on, but they had feeble collective nerve. The punch I saw one of them throw barely grazed Viktor's shoulder.

I left my partner to figure out how we ought best to proceed. I told her what little I'd learned about Kenny and his Ford, had a look at the man himself once rent-a-cop had pointed him out. Then I handed my partner the reins, by which I mean I asked her, "So?"

"Be a shame if they killed him," she told me back and added presently, "I guess."

I was about as sold on that as she was. A shame for Viktor certainly, and maybe for client Sue a little if she ran into a boy toy shortage, but it was difficult to think of a world without Viktor in it as shortchanged.

"Did he come to hurt her? Naomi?" I wanted to know.

My partner shook her head. "If we give him the rocks, he goes back home."

"Do we even know what they're worth?"

She shrugged. "Enough to bring him here."

"That's not them. That's Uri," I said. "Viktor wants to keep his fingers."

"They're kind of Russell's rocks now," is what my partner floated.

"He doesn't want them," I told her. "Uri'd work on him as well."

"Fine, but when I settle with Dottie, I'll need a quarter inch."

I tried to calculate how much of Byron's money a quarter inch would be, but I was still a touch too rummy for that kind of math.

"All right, I guess. What about him?"

Viktor and those boys were still tussling.

"Well," she said, "if he found Naomi once, maybe he can do it again."

I nodded, and my partner reached down and pulled her .38 out of her ankle holster, raised it up, and fired three shots in the air.

The racket had the intended effect. The scrum went still and silent. A few of those boys even gave ground enough to leave a gap where my partner could wade in. She grabbed Viktor by an ear and pulled him out.

Those scrum boys made a show of powerful disappointment like they would have gotten around to homicide in time.

Viktor, for his part, winked at my partner as an expression, I guess, of gratitude. Then he displayed the tip of his tongue because he was short of self-awareness and seemed prepared to believe my partner was weak against his magnetism. It's possible he suspected she'd heard talk of his technique.

We made him ride in the trunk because the rest of us all had a touch of sandalwood poisoning. Since my partner appeared to know the county like a local, I was content to let her take charge.

"What's the plan?" I asked her.

"We drop them," she told me, "and then pull Viktor out and put him to work." She pointed at the glovebox and said my way, "Quarter-inch. Nothing less."

So I pulled out Byron's envelope and did some guesstimating. It didn't amount to gemstone money but wasn't bad for just riding around. I handed it back to rent-a-cop who didn't even count it but just gave it straight to her mister who appeared to sniff it for a while.

I suddenly felt optimistic and at ease enough to chat up rent-a-cop for a bit and make a point of thanking the woman for sluicing me off in the motel tub.

"Couldn't have been pretty," is what I said.

She told me back that she'd seen worse and turned her head to have a piercing look at her mister. He'd left off sniffing Byron's money and so was free to give her quarter minute of haughty pig Latin back.

Those two lived about where I would have guessed, out in

a shabby subdivision with a rusty dumpster at the head of the road. It looked like most of that subdivision had given up on simple maintenance, and folks throughout were using their front yards to park assorted stuff. Cars they'd stopped driving. Lawn mowers they'd never fix. Furniture not really manufactured to sit in the rain. Appliances too of about every stripe, and quite a lot of rugrat clutter.

I guess rent-a-cop noticed me soaking all of it in.

"Used to be nice," she told me, "back before folks got tired."

Their house and grounds were pretty much average. A Cub Cadet with two tires, a lawn chair with no webbing, and three or four bags of trash that might reach the dumpster eventually.

I thought we were only going to drop them off and then get to work with Viktor who kept reminding us he was in the trunk with muffled commentary and surprisingly tart cologne. When we stopped in front of rent-a-cop's house, I noticed a bird on her roof.

"That your duck?" I asked her.

Once she'd discharged all the breath she could, she told me back, "I guess."

She and her mister climbed out, my partner as well, and the three of them went up the walk together. Rent-a-cop's mister struggled towards the stairs while my partner and rent-a-cop stayed in the yard and talked.

I was hoping for a quick goodbye, but they chatted and then chatted some more. When I blew the horn a couple of times, it was partly as a joke, but I was also past ready to find Naomi and make the long drive south. There was a group that met at the Church of Christ around the corner from where I lived, and I knew if I managed to keep fairly straight all the way back home, that bunch downstairs at the fellowship hall would help me stay on the beam in a way that my partner would never be able to touch.

I blew the horn another time, and that's what brought the neighbor out.

"Hey!" He said as he came stalking over.

The man was underdressed and tattooed, bloated and puffy, and by the time he'd reached the Chevrolet, he'd spelled something at me twice.

Rent-a-cop said a few things to him from over in the yard, but he still lingered by the Chevrolet to natter at me further. I couldn't imagine what he was steamed about. The man was coming off like a nut.

I might not have been at my best, but I still wasn't about to take guff from a civilian, so I rolled out of the Chevy to do some jawing back. The guy retreated into the street when he saw me coming, and he ended up in front of an SUV that was rolling up the block. It was a big shiny black one with tinted windows that stopped to give him a chance to move clear.

He didn't and wouldn't but stayed where he was and spelled at me another time. That earned him a blast from the SUV horn, so he spelled at it as well until it jolted forward and knocked him onto the asphalt.

The driver's door swung open, and out came a man I immediately recognized. He was big and square and had one tattered ear. The two times I'd arrested his brother, he'd been the one to bail him out. "'Lo Gleb," is what I told him.

As he grabbed a handful of the neighbor, Gleb had a glance my way and said back, "Oh" and "Hey."

MISTER

The words usually sound all right in my head but come out so slobbered up that even I can hardly tell just what I'm saying, so it isn't like I can blame her for not listening anymore.

Her real estate lady called two nights before my fit. I happened to hear the message she left and so knew what Dottie was planning. I still wonder why she didn't pack up and follow through. I certainly wouldn't have stuck around to do the stuff she's doing just because I'd sworn an oath and felt betrothed. She feeds me and wipes me and washes me down, works the job I used to work. I guess Dottie's hoping I'll come around just enough to let her leave.

I'll never know exactly why Doug could understand me. He laid it off to the dent in his head, or to the crease in his brain his dent had made that gave him (he told me) a few peculiar powers. Aside from sussing me out, Doug claimed he could bend aluminum by staring at it and identify Episcopalians from their smell. I never saw him get up to either of those, but when I'd pop off with something slushy, Doug always knew exactly what I meant.

That was refreshing for me since everybody else seemed to think I was daft, had something badly wrong with my tongue, or might possibly be Belgian. Doug, though, would answer my questions to him, enlarge upon my points, and engage me in the brand of give and take I'd not enjoyed since my fit.

What I learned from Doug at bottom was I didn't have a mystery. I had some shrubbery trash on our back bedroom wall and the contents of a lunchbox that he'd tossed aside because he'd been upset in a particular way.

"Itchy twitchy," is how Doug put it.

Doug had what he called nervous troubles that would build up in him for some time and then release in a kind of spurt. He seemed to believe he'd committed manslaughter during one of his spasms, and he told me he woke up once in a house lying next to an ancient lady who called him Boyd and was wearing only her upper teeth and a corset. Doug couldn't remember how he got there and still didn't know who she was.

I heard from Doug the high points of his incarceration. He'd gone in for violence against his family and harm to one of the neighbor girls. "That bunch," he told me, "was really hard to take."

Doug had served his time in a hospital for criminal nuts and hopeless cases, and he said he'd taken a sort of cure from a doctor in the place. She had a sinus complaint, and she made quite a lot of respirational racket that Doug found soothing somehow and therapeutic.

"Funny world, isn't it," is what Doug told me. "She gave me pills, but I didn't need to take them. Her breathing was enough."

We connected, me and Doug because he didn't simply tolerate me the way most everybody else did. They'd grin and nod when I said a thing, would look tempted to pat my head. But Doug heard me out and chatted back, so when he said he had to go, I persuaded him to let me tag along.

I didn't figure Dottie would worry much. She's not the fretting sort. I'd gotten worked up a few times before and had struck out on my own but usually didn't get more than a half-mile from the house except for once when I caught a ride with some girls who drove me across the county. They'd decided I was retarded and needed an afternoon of fun. That came to mean two cans of Milwaukee's Best and a bra rubbed in my face.

They eventually dropped me off at the permanent yard sale way out on the Mechanicsville road, which was a feedlot full of third-hand junk that a guy who'd lost interest in cattle operated and oversaw. He called Dottie for me, and when she drove out to fetch me, she bought an iron skillet and a couple of slotted spoons.

I was never much of a catch myself, and by the time I landed Dottie, I was built like a hatrack and maybe half as charming. She was a cute brunette in those days who wouldn't have settled for me if her fiance hadn't thrown her over for a spunky Christian woman. Dottie needed something with a scrotum to get back at him, and I happened to be handy and willing as far as it went.

So she was better than I rated, and I knew that from the jump, which left me feeling more suspicious than lucky because I couldn't trust a woman who looked like Dottie did but was running around with me. To her credit, she wasn't affectionate except out in public every now and then when she'd decided there was a chance her fiance might run across us. Times I'd get her alone and snuggle up to show her what I was thinking, she'd usually give me a peck and a shove and say, "Get off."

We were never unhappy exactly, but we were never happy either. I know she didn't grow to love me, and I cooled to her over time. We were less like husband and wife than colleagues in bad careers who happened to take meals together and lived under the same roof.

I had a girlfriend for a little while. Dottie didn't exactly drive me to her, but she'd made it plain by then there'd be no tenderness between us, so I fell in briefly with a lady I knew from work. I got her on the rebound from a guy she'd met at the drugstore. They'd hooked up in the ointment aisle where he'd advised her on a rash.

For her part, Lori simply had needs, and most men around were attached to the gear she required. There was precious little a fellow could do or say to put her off, but that also meant we lacked the means to keep her since Lori knew she could find what she wanted just about anywhere she pleased. I didn't, consequently, romance the woman but chiefly took my turn. We had a go in my car and a couple of afternoons in her apartment.

Then a new neighbor moved in upstairs from Lori, and she went to work on him.

I had my stroke one week to the day after my last meet up with Lori, and I came around in the ER sure I was suffering the judgment of the Lord. I was alone in one of those cubicles where they'd drawn a curtain around me, and I had a clip on my finger, a tube up my nose, and a needle in my arm. I felt scared and confused, and I tried to yell to bring somebody to me, which is when I discovered nothing much still worked. I'd only gotten as far as grunting and gurgling when Dottie parted the curtains and came in.

She didn't take my hand or anything but informed me I'd had a stroke and regurgitated a few choice items she'd heard from a nurse or a doctor. "They figure you'll live," she told me. "Might get all right in time."

With that, she looked me up and down. "Move what you can," she told me.

I made an attempt, but everything stayed where it was.

So I left the house in the middle of the night, went off riding with Doug who we only knew because he'd thrown a lunchbox in a bush and then had followed Dottie home once she'd confessed to him she had it. As best I could tell, the only item Doug cared to retrieve was a sandwich sack with five brass buttons in it.

"Been in your family?" I asked him. I hoped I'd hear an explanation of why those buttons had drawn Doug all the way to the house, but he just shoved them in his pocket and told me, "No."

Doug's car was a mess. Lose stuff everywhere. Papers and clothes and drive-thru rubbish scattered thick around. There was a gap for the driver that Doug slipped into and then left me to clear a slot for myself. I had to move mail mostly, and I could see it was addressed to all sorts of people who weren't necessarily Doug. Some of them were local, but a bunch were down in cackalacky and Georgia.

Doug caught me eyeing an envelope. "Yeah," he told me, "I'm

bad about that."

I didn't know exactly what he meant until we'd gone about three blocks when Doug veered across the road to a mailbox. Its door was off, and some puckered, weathered mail was laying inside. He helped himself to what looked like pizza fliers and car loan come-ons. Doug barely glanced at the stuff before he flung it into the back.

"Got to," he told me. "Can't really say why. Look there."

Doug pointed at a mailbox just two driveways up. Somebody had gone to the bother to attach the thing to an antique garden plow, but the box was dented and rusty, and there was bulk mail sticking out. He grabbed all that and flung it behind him as well.

People get wrought up over all grades of stuff. I used to have a thing about my side view mirrors and could never get them pitched and angled to suit me, so I felt like I understood Doug a little and was prepared to believe we had a meaningful thing or two in common, especially once you'd set his dent and his years in the nuthouse aside.

We didn't, in fact, go anywhere special but just toured around the county. Occasionally Doug would weary of driving and pull off the road and park. He was partial to church lots, and sometimes he'd climb up onto the roof of the car where he'd strip down to his underpants and do a kind of jig for a while.

His sedan sure suffered for it. It was a Dodge from way back with a couple of cracks in the windshield and a concave roof.

When I asked him how he liked his car, by way of making conversation, Doug responded with a snatch of Scripture. At least I think that's what it was, and then he wondered what I thought of a man who'd have his way with a child.

"Not much, I guess," I told him.

"And then she turns out rotten. There's not a lot that goes on in this life that doesn't lead to something else."

I didn't know what he meant exactly, but I was getting used to that since there was little about Doug that was regular and normal. I had to think he'd started odd, and then the nuthouse hadn't helped because he'd twitch and snort, even yelp a little in between bouts of doing nothing or saying curious things. So while I was pleased enough to be out of the house and gratified to have for company a man who understood me, I was still having an odd time of it because of the brand of thing Doug was.

That's how it went until morning. We did all kinds of starting and stopping until Doug pulled into a trailer park out where I'd never been before and took special interest in a yellow van parked there. It had tin patches on some rust spots and was yellow only mostly because it looked like whoever had done the work had either run out of gumption or paint.

When I asked Doug what we were up to, I got back one of his grunts, the kind I took to mean that I should sit still and say nothing. Doug had an expressive way with racket from his neck. We spent a good half hour watching that van and the man who came and went from it. He looked like he hadn't glanced at a mirror in a while because he was messy and undone in ways you could fix if you knew about it. Hair standing funny. Shirt buttoned wrong. Fly half up and one trouser leg in a boot.

"Know him?"

Another grunt.

I like a mystery far too much for a grunt to hold me long. "Do you?"

"We stayed there," Doug said and pointed with his dent primarily at the sky blue trailer the man kept coming out of and then going back into.

That raised even more questions, but before I could begin to go at Doug, a guy rolled our way on a bike and hit us with concentrated palaver. He was talking as he reached us and kept up a solid stream of yack after he'd stopped alongside the driver's door where he visited chatter on Doug before turning his notice my way and asking Doug about me as well. He kept talking while he licked his fingers and smeared some dirt across his chest. He looked the sort who kept his shirt off from probably Easter to Halloween.

Doug didn't do much talking back, but then he wasn't really required to because the boy on the bike would soon get around to answering all the questions he asked.

"Where'd y'all get off to? Word around is you're staying up by Dooley's. His sister (she's dead now, Betty or something) lived with a woman out near Cullen, all queer and stuff, you know? Fine by me, if that's what you want." He paused to discharge snot and then had a glance my way as he was dragging the back of his hand across his nose. "Do I know him? Think I might somehow."

Doug grunted and got ignored.

"Who you?"

I began to assure the guy he didn't know me and was maybe halfway through it when I met with cause to remember that Doug was the only one around with a gift.

"Where's he even from?" That boy seemed openly disgusted.

Doug grunted another time and directed that boy's attention to the man between the yellow van and the sky blue trailer. He was standing still and looked to be trying to recall if he was going or coming.

"Rico," the boy said. "Thinks y'all still live here. I didn't tell him different."

We all watched Rico walk to his van like a man wading through oatmeal. He slid open the side door and sat down hard.

The boy leaned in to speak to Doug exclusively. I was too foreign to rate his notice. "Somebody put him on you," is what he said. "All he does is blow stuff up."

So we waited Rico out and then followed him, which proved no simple thing to do because he poked along and sat at junctions, would ease off the side of the road every now and again to linger a bit. If I'd been him, I would have noticed us lurking around behind him, but he didn't seem to and led us in time to a farm in the middle of nothing much where he took his van down a rocky track and around to an old hay barn.

I was fairly well engaged by then because I'm a man who likes a mystery and here we were after a fellow who was said to blow stuff up. I kept waiting for Doug to fill me in on details and backstory but instead, he said nothing and stayed on the road until he'd found an empty church lot where he climbed onto the roof of his Dodge and had a nearly naked prance.

I got out of the car and parked myself off alongside a light pole just in case that Dodge was good and ready to let Doug sink on through.

There wasn't any useful talking to Doug about immediate plans and tactics because he was too fixed on larger complaints for that. He especially had regrets about some woman in his life that he never got past calling her and she.

"Riboflavin," Doug said three or four times over. He seemed to think it the root of his troubles because he wouldn't have been where he was but for needing to go and read boxes and cans.

It turned out Doug's girl had nudged him into stuff he thought he'd put behind him. She'd touched off and brought out bad behavior Doug had believed he'd curbed, and he told me again about his doctor with the deviated septum who had calmed and cured him by the way she breathed.

"Truth be told," Doug said as he came off the roof and onto the hood, "I'm more than a little disappointed in me."

Doug put his clothes back on and drove us over near that barn again, but there was a Pontiac parked on the roadside in the one wide spot that wasn't a ditch. It was low slung and blue/black and dusty and had a Florida license tag. The mere sight of the thing appeared to give Doug a bout of indigestion, and as we rolled past it to a place where Doug could turn around, he said maybe three or four times just, "Lord."

Doug found a place to park by a gulley where folks threw out their old TVs and tires along with the odd water heater and electric stove. That's how it works out in the country. Some intrepid soul will locate a weedy sinkhole his Amana will fit into, and the fact of it peeking out ever so slightly from kudzu will attract other people riding the roads with appliances to dump.

"I can't get through there," I told Doug.

He was eyeing a route between two belted radials and a Frigidaire. "Can too," he told me, and damned if he didn't pick me up off the ground and carry me down from the road and into that gulley.

On the way up the other side, he only dropped me twice. I barely got dinged up and only a little grimy, and then we ended up fighting our way through a hedgerow and crossing an overgrown pasture where the grass and the weeds were high enough to keep us hidden from the barn.

"Who's in the Pontiac?" I asked Doug while we were resting and hunkering down, and just then a guy came walking out of the barn and up the track toward the road.

"Him," Doug told me. "Things sure get tangled up sometimes." I waited for more, but he left it at that.

As we closed on that barn, I reminded Doug twice, "I'm not looking to get blown up."

Doug told me he was happy to go in alone, and that was fine with me since, aside from disabled, I'm nobody's brave man too.

I stayed out near a pile of trash, lots of wiring and switches and mess, and didn't have to wait long for Doug to come out of that old hay barn and join me.

He grabbed my good hand, laid a toe on my palm, and said nothing except, "Here."

None of it was making any sense to me. We'd just been riding the roads for a while with a guy in the trunk who stank like a funeral wreath and a guy up front who smelled a bit like a cow lot.

I'd decided by then that folding cash would serve us better than jewels since keeping the various things we'd found was proving a bit of a problem. Doug had already walked away with the buttons, big brass things with a sailing boat on them, and stinky in the trunk was going to leave with the rocks because his boss, they'd told us, would make us suffer for keeping them anyway.

Bossman, they said, was a truly bent rascal given to easy violence. I'd had an uncle like that. My mother's least brother who'd pinch my leg or bite me or knock me over when nobody was around.

"Kind of a nut," is what stinky told us. "Won't be leaving you room to explain." He looked to haircut for confirmation, and she backed him with a nod.

Since we'd recently seen that man on a motel room floor sprawled in his own leakage, he needed whatever support and affirmation he could get.

I asked what they had planned for the guy we were hauling in the trunk, but nobody understood me. They looked to Dottie, like folks do, but she'd stopped listening ages back. Stinky had a way of trying to tell me what he thought I'd said, which was always wrong, and he'd do it loud and slow and then add, "Right?" like I was some geezer who didn't know supper from lunch.

They all get around in time to wanting to hear if I'm right

in the head, but they always put it to Dottie because they can't imagine I'd know. I do know, though, since I'm more tuned into me than most of them think. If Doug had been handy, I'd have let him tell them for me that I'm tweaked. Not damaged but more in the way of differently organized. My nose works better than it used to, a good thing but for stinky and smelly. I can see better too, but I've got a fairly constant buzz in my ears, and the muscles in my weak leg tend to knot up and plague me. I can't make the fingers of my bad hand do much of anything. I've not gone stupid, though, no matter how the drooling looks.

It seemed to me we'd done a bunch of traveling around to find out awfully little, and you hardly needed to be a brainiac to recognize that. But it sounded like stinky and haircut and smelly guy in the trunk still had many miles ahead of them yet. I'd fairly well lost interest in the entire business by then, was even hungry for a couple of jars of baby food chicken, which meant I was keen to get in the house once haircut had pulled up out front and stopped.

It didn't transpire that way, however, because haircut wanted to talk to Dottie and so kind of held us up on the front walk where she apologized for her stinky partner and thanked Dottie for all her help. Dottie was doing her bit to drag things out by thanking haircut for the payday when stinky decided he'd had enough and started blowing the car horn.

Naturally, that brought Clarence out, and he spelled Eletriptan at us, which stinky didn't appear to give a toss about.

Then a big black car came rolling up and nudged Clarence right on over. The driver climbed out, stepped up to Clarence and told him a thing or two. Clarence complained at high volume while the SUV driver and haircut's stinky partner nodded hey.

"Friend of yours?" I asked haircut, but she couldn't tell what I said and just stood there watching that fellow climb back into his big black car and then ease into the ditch ahead of their Chevy. The driver got out another time and opened the near back door.

A man climbed out in the company of a girl.

I heard haircut say, "Hmm." I heard haircut tell Dottie, "This might be a problem."

The guy from the backseat hardly looked as much trouble as the one behind the wheel. He had both of his ears and was dressed for maybe a date at the Olive Garden. The girl with him, though, she was an odd sight, all done up like a baby doll. A girly frock and frilly socks and shiny buckled shoes. Her hair was shiny too and laying funny like somebody had given her wig a quarter turn. Her face was pale except for a spot on one cheek where she had a coming bruise.

Olive Garden had her by the arm and not in a fond endearing way but with one of those grips that would let him jerk and haul her around as he pleased.

He smiled as he spoke to stinky, glanced at Clarence, had a look up our street. He struck me as one of those guys prone to stay amused over how some people choose to live and what they elect to get up to, and when I say amused I mean disgusted but with a show of teeth.

Stinky clearly knew him just like he knew bad ear guy as well.

"Who are they?" I asked haircut who, naturally, didn't understand me, but before she could inquire of Dottie what I might have said, her partner opened the trunk of the Chevy, and smelly Viktor popped up. Then him and Olive Garden had kind of a conversation.

Shortly thereafter, haircut happened in fact to answer my question. She told Dottie anyway, "Uri. Viktor's boss. They'd be his rocks."

"He looks all right." I could tell exactly what Dottie intended by the tone she took. She meant it was nice to see a man who'd taken some care with his clothes and was capable of having a chat in the street while he kept a woman in hand. She didn't need to swing around and have a look my way for me to be aware of the comparison she was making.

I muttered a thing Dottie's way it was just as well she couldn't decipher, and then me and her and haircut together watched Olive Garden turn Clarence's way and kick him viciously twice.

I have to think Clarence had spelled Eletriptan a couple of times too many, and Olive Garden had ignored him at it for as long as he could bear. Then Clarence turned his volume up. That was a habit with him. Clarence has a knack for bringing your patience with him to an end.

Olive Garden, from what I could see, was a strategic, effective kicker, and even though he appeared to be wearing only loafers, he found two tender places with them and shut Clarence right on up. And it was like he hardly noticed what he was was doing. He went straight back to chatting with stinky. I could tell they were talking about the girl from the way she got jerked around.

Olive Garden had this way of seeming capable of all grades of grim, unsavory stuff. It had nothing to do with what he said. Instead, he looked like a man who couldn't be bothered to care much about people or trouble himself over what became of the ones who'd get in his way. It was all in that toothy grin of disgust and eyes like you'd find on a ground snake. I was well across the yard and up the walk, but I was even scared of him from there.

Viktor in the trunk looked like he was with me. He was talking too fast and working too hard to make everything seem ok. He appeared to be telling an elaborate story, was doing it out of fear is how it looked. He kept pointing at the girl in the baby doll clothes and holding forth about her in some way.

"Naomi," haircut explained to Dottie. "The girl Kelvin's running with." She troubled herself to explain my way, "Doug."

From where I was standing, she didn't look much of a catch and hardly the sort to be all that persuasive, but I had to think Olive Garden had let some air out of the girl. She was standing there with her arm gripped tight and enduring Viktor's comments. She kept glancing at the guy with the tattered ear because he was within arm's reach as well, and her being dressed like a baby doll made it all the weirder. We seemed to be an awfully long way from a pink lunchbox in a shrub.

It was hard to know what might happen, though it looked in that moment to me like everything was lining up to be bad for the girl. Olive Garden had her. Stinky partner wanted her. She'd put smelly Viktor in a tight spot with those boys out at the rink, and I knew from Doug that she was the one who'd set him on a spree when he'd just hoped to keep cutting grass and maintain his riboflavin.

She'd gotten knocked around already. That was easy enough to see, and whenever bad ear guy made a move, she twitched and quivered.

None of that meant I still wasn't hungry, something close to famished. I was a grown man fairly jonesing for baby mush, so my thinking wasn't as unobstructed as it might have been since I half wanted to know what was going on but half wanted to fill my piehole. That left me more impatient and distracted than I otherwise would have been. Ill too, I should say. Just generally peeved, which accounts for why I decided to pop off.

That bunch was chatting by the Chevrolet when Clarence raised a fuss again. He was still in the street laying flat on his back like some kind of tattooed turtle, and he started making noises about the cop he ought to call. Of course, he spelled Eletriptan a fair few times more but kept circling back around to the police in a way that even I could tell would not be helpful to him. That was well before Olive Garden gave his head a shake and looked around from the girl to the guy in the trunk to haircut's smelly partner as if to ask them just by pulling a face what a fellow like him should do when a grown man was displaying the nerve to threaten him with the police.

I shouted for Clarence to shut his mouth, and I think that saved him briefly, that and the fact that the girl noticed we had a duck up on our roof.

"Would you look," she said and pointed with the arm he wasn't holding, but Olive Garden didn't come across as the sort to distinguish among birds.

He glanced toward the roof and then glared my way. He put

to stinky partner the usual question, which was if there was something wrong with me or if I was just from France.

"Had a fit of some kind." I could hear him from where I stood.

Past himself, Olive Garden didn't much care about the human condition and so lost interest in me immediately and gave ear guy possession of the girl. That freed him up to address himself to Clarence in a wholesale way.

He came across as a man who kicked and stomped his path through life in just one gear. That's what I remember thinking anyway as Olive Garden laid into Clarence, first with the toe of his loafer, then the heel of his loafer and even his knee a couple of times.

I don't believe he ever said anything, and he didn't seem particularly angry. A threat had been made against him, and he was duty-bound to respond. So while there was harm to deliver, there was no need to be hot about it. That's what made him scary, even from a distance. While Olive Garden tore up Clarence, he stayed dead cool.

I thought at first stinky partner might feel obliged to intervene, to put himself between Olive Garden's foot and Clarence, but he stayed right where he was while Olive Garden did his damage and only spoke up once things were winding down.

"I think he hears you," is what stinky partner said.

Clarence was busted to bits by then and was rolling around on the pavement. He was bleeding and moaning and in dire shape as best I could tell.

I guess Olive Garden didn't like the way I was looking from him to Clarence and then from Clarence back to him because he turned up his volume and said my way just, "Problem?"

I felt bold enough in the moment to tell him that Clarence wasn't any sort of threat but just a mouthy neighbor who got headaches. It all came out as garbled primate noises, the brand of racket that would have let the air out of most anybody else's irritation, but Olive Garden wasn't compassionate that way, so he kept on glaring at me even after Dottie had called out to him that I was off in the head, had the brains of a child, and made racket day and night that didn't actually mean much of anything.

Stinky partner endorsed that explanation, but Olive Garden still glared my way and told me I'd better be off in the head. Then he took hold of baby doll again and jerked her hard by the arm.

I hadn't stood up for decency in such a long time that I didn't quite know what I was feeling. I'd opted for a load of self-pity day and night for nearly a year, so genuine indignation didn't come off as familiar, especially since I had no use for Clarence and didn't even know the girl. Maybe on another day and at another time I would have rooted for a man who'd had enough of Clarence to stomp him hard, but Olive Garden hit me wrong. I didn't like a thing about him.

Part of it was the violence and the way he gripped the girl, but I also didn't like how he buffed his loafers on the backs of his pant legs and the way he looked at Dottie and us like he could barely stand the sight.

I told him something further. That's how put out I was. I said I didn't much care for the way he was treating folks on my own street.

"Now what?" Olive Garden asked in a general way. He seemed to be seeking a proper translation.

I didn't like the look he shot me and so told him a thing or three more.

"You're pushing it, friend," is what he said back.

"He's not right," haircut told him.

"Sometimes you don't need to hear what a man says to know what he's talking about."

I got even angrier from having to endure his folksy philosophy, and I guess Dottie could see I was cocked and ready to uncork more palaver, so she headed me off by poking me and telling me, "Pssst."

When I looked her way, she jerked her nose in the direction of the house, and I decided I knew precisely what she had in mind for me to do. It's funny how that works sometimes – dead sure and yet all wrong.

So I fought my way up the stairs to the porch, hauling myself along the rail, and I'm certain haircut and Dottie were pointing out how halt and feeble I was just in case Olive Garden was still half itching to stomp me, and then I was in the house and out of his sight and headed straight down the hall.

The thing might have been in pieces, but once I'd slapped it back together, it looked persuasive enough. I even had a bullet I kept in Dottie's bedside drawer, and I dug it out and got it into the cylinder after a while. Then I practiced holding the parts together so that pistol looked half lethal.

I caught sight of myself in the mirror and snarled something manly that came out sounding like gas.

BIG BROTHER

i

We weren't friends. He was six years younger and would do all sorts of things I never would have done. Arson for money. Arms running. A touch of piracy. He even came to me for a loan once and used it to romance my ex in Baku. They rolled around by the Caspian Sea for the best part of a week. Later on, he sought my forgiveness and showed me where she'd bit him, which he allowed he'd thought he might enjoy but didn't in the end.

My little brother wasn't slick, but he was bold and more than a bit of a charmer. He was the sort who thought looking a month ahead was taking the long view. For my part, I plan and plod and have little use for people, so even a meager dusting of charm would have probably been wasted on me. Our older brother was worse than that. He'd come out of the mine to sleep and drink when he wasn't smacking our mother around. When the methane blew and he died down there, none of us really cared. We did, though, miss his regular money, so I went off to be an earner.

I caught on with a guy in Tbilisi for a little over a year and made a name for myself by punishing people for him. Usually with my fists alone, occasionally with a hammer, but I got sloppy with one rascal and let him bite off half my ear. I pounded him for it, naturally, a little more than was required. When he failed to recover, I got sent away to greater Miami and worked for my old boss's cousin there. He ran used car lots as a front for shifting flesh and moving drugs. The girls came in on boats from Mexico, the drugs on boats from Cuba, but I didn't have to mess with any of that because I just drove the man around.

He had a wife and several girlfriends, and a couple of them had husbands. Consequently, he kept me close at hand in case some trouble kicked off. Of course, there were drug-running and flesh-peddling rivals he had to be mindful of as well, so it got to where I went pretty much wherever he needed to go, which involved a lot of sitting outside of restaurants and hotels. I read magazines to work on my English and practiced being serene.

That made for kind of an apprenticeship with my Tbilisi boss's cousin, and I got myself in shape for stepping up to a bigger boss. It wasn't, though, like I could slip around and look for a new position, so I had to wait for the chance to show off my skills. I got it once my guy met with trouble from a lady who was cleaning money for him and also skimming off the top. She needed the cash to pay another man she'd skimmed off of as well who'd found her out and had dispatched one of her house cats with a machete.

She blubbered the details to my boss once he'd caught her stealing as well. She still owed money to machete man, and she had a second cat, so she was all kinds of nervous about what might happen to him and a little upset about what might happen to her. Luckily, she impressed my bossman as potential girlfriend material. He liked them bony and blonde and bronze from the sun, and she ticked every box in addition to being needy, which meant she wouldn't require romancing. He'd do for her, and she'd do for him back.

My boss proposed he take a meeting with the other man she'd cheated who'd be expecting that girl and a chunk of money but would get my boss and an explanation instead. It seemed chancy to me, but I was fairly deep in serenity by then and so held my opinion close and only drove. My boss practiced his spiel along the way. He tried out assorted approaches and ended up flatly insisting the other guy ease up on the girl and, while he was at it, lay off her remaining cat.

We met the man in the parking lot of one of those big box stores gone bust with an interstate a hundred yards away and boggy swamp everywhere else.

He was waiting for us in a big beige Escalade, or waiting any-way for his leggy money launderer who owed him thirty-two large. He had a man with him – driver and muscle – and they both climbed out as we entered the lot and rolled up.

I left the car and opened the door for my boss who buttoned his blazer and tugged at his sleeves like he was heading for a cocktail. The guy across the way shrugged as if to say, "Who in the name of our Lord are you?"

My boss took a few steps in that fellow's direction.

The guy rubbed a thumb and forefinger together. "Money?" is what he said.

My boss raised a finger in a hold-on-a-sec kind of way.

It turned out the gentleman by the Cadillac had a pronounced impatient streak, and he immediately gave instructions to his muscle who came lumbering our way, so I met with the chance to show off what I could do.

He was the cornfed sort, a big ropey lunk who would have made you sorry you'd ever drawn breath if he hit you. Big *if* though because there was too much of him to move with speed or grace. He came stalking our way like a yak in a suit, and my boss backed up to clear some real estate for me. Up to that point, he'd only ever seen me take care of wiry, druggy sorts along with the occasional management type gone plush. This man was something else entirely and looked perfectly capable of turning us into stew beef if we didn't stop him first.

If I didn't stop him, that is to say. So I made a plan as he ap-proached. Like I said, I'm strategic, unlike my little brother, which meant by the time that sack of meat reached me, I was organized to put him down.

He wanted to shove and punch and wrestle, wrench my joints apart, so I just stayed out of his reach while I found his tender places. There wasn't much challenge to it since he was too mus-cle-heavy to move. I'm no gazelle myself, but I had little trouble circling and dodging and then planting long enough to deliver punishing, level blows. The first few didn't appear to faze him much, but I softened him up in time. I eventually broke his nose to blind him, and a short, sharp punch in the throat put him down. That made it a cinch to boot him in vulnerable spots and keep him on the ground.

He was sprawled and bloody and barely moving by the time my boss came out from behind our car.

I feared he might gloat, but instead, he asked the guy across the way if he was ready for a conversation now that the preliminaries were well and truly out of the way.

I half expected that man to climb into his Escalade and lock the doors, but he walked straight over to us. He was a slacks and polo shirt sort and so hardly seemed much of a danger until you looked into his eyes. There was something decidedly off about him that workplace casual couldn't hide.

My boss started in on his skimming blonde and how she needed a bit of time to work off her obligations. He made an open appeal to that fellow's sense of money-laundering decency, but the guy didn't appear to be listening to my boss much at all. Instead, he was sizing up the damage I'd done to his driver who was still sprawled and moaning on the ground.

When he finally spoke, he was talking to me. "Where'd you learn all that?"

I told him, "Around," but he shook his head and motioned that I should get specific, so I said I'd picked it up from roughnecks in the motherland, most especially a Croat I'd worked with as a bouncer who was self-taught and (when he wanted to be) as lethal as a blade.

That was enough for Escalade guy. He picked out a couple of spots on his driver's torso where he could fit a loafer and then kicked and stomped the man for what felt like an uneasy while.

He didn't do it with anger but more in the way of energetic resolve and kept it up until my boss man said, "All right."

For a few seconds there I thought Escalade guy might stomp my boss man a bit as well, but instead, he wiped his shoes on his pants and told me, "I'll give you twice what you're getting from him."

"Hold on."

He ignored my boss man. "Unless you want to keep driving him to skanks."

My old boss man spluttered. My new boss man winked. Then he turned and headed back to his car and never checked to see if I was coming. He'd gotten enough of a read on me to be sure of the direction I would take.

I drove that Escalade to a swanky condo down along the beach and sat and waited while my new boss went inside. He took a machete with him. He didn't try to hide it but carried it like you might a riding crop.

He was gone maybe ten minutes altogether and then came back down and climbed back in. He gave me directions to a steakhouse up the beach at Sunny Isles. I'd driven maybe a mile or two when my new boss wondered at me if I could account why anybody in this wide world would own a cat.

I didn't find out who he actually was until the following morning, though I'd heard enough about the local criminal element to know to narrow my choices. He had to be Uri or a Czech who worked out of Pompano and was notorious for his sadistic streak.

I only figured it out for certain once I'd heard him talk to a waitress who he called *Sugar* and *Bubbula* both at once and together. I was relieved. That Czech was a wild man while Uri was merely ruthless but known to be highly organized and goal-oriented as well. He only ever gave you what you'd earned but did it without exception.

For a long time, I liked him, or something in the vicinity of it. He was calm and certain and paid every other Thursday with cash. Primarily, I drove. Uri worked out of his car. He had a house in Broward, nothing special, just a ranch in a suburb. I never went inside, but you could see in from the road. He didn't even have curtains up. Nothing on the walls. No furniture much.

The talk was he'd had a girlfriend once, some sort of regular lady who was slow to detect what a dark bit of business he was. She backed off, of course, once she'd found him out like any normal human would.

I did tasks for him aside from driving, but instead of thrashing people who'd crossed him or gone into arrears, chiefly I just held folks down and worked to stay clear, there at first, of his machete, but soon enough he shifted to snips.

He got his first pair off of a man who owed him fourteen thousand dollars. The guy was some kind of builder who'd had a big contract fall through, and he was wearing those snips in a holster when we finally caught up with him. I held him down on an upended joint compound bucket while Uri reacquainted them with his terms and was raising the usual level of panic by waving around his machete when he noticed the snips in the holster and drew them out for a look.

That builder might have been a poor businessman, but he took splendid care of his tools, and that pair of tin snips he was hauling around had been lovingly oiled and maintained. It looked like he'd lately redipped the grips and put a fresh edge on the blades. There was no rust anywhere, no greasy gunk, just dark steel with a dull sheen and fresh red rubber to hold.

They spoke to Uri, that pair of snips. He admired them in silence for a bit before dropping his machete and announcing with something like breathy rapture, "Now these..."

That was Uri all over. The man always had time for attentive appreciation. He'd see this or that thing out in the world and stop what he was up to for a spot of admiration. Uri especially championed craftsmanship, and I had more than once waited while Uri soaked in some graceful stonework or impeccably executed joinery. He seemed to like to acknowledge the fine, noble things that people could get up to before he punished some associate for letting his species down.

That was Uri all over, yin and yang. I think he'd long since convinced himself he only got up to what he had to, and it might have even pained him a little to lop off fingers, earlobes, and toes. He certainly didn't take open pleasure in it like that nut from Pompano.

Those snips were better for him all around, and he recognized it immediately. They'd readily slip into his pocket. They were razor-sharp and easy to clean. The works were smooth, and – given the build and the leverage – they passed through flesh and bone with relative ease. Next to a machete, those snips were little short of elegant, and Uri plainly preferred to be the guy who lopped rather than hacked.

"I'll tell you this, colonel," he said to me more than once, "we're all done or undone by the little things."

He would prove in the end to be a prophet where it came to that.

So I was happy in my work, which is all anybody can hope for. I drove Uri. I held his clients down so he could instruct them however he needed, and he kept us in fresh vehicles. We got a new SUV every three months. Uri had a soft spot for the smell of a car just off the line.

For me, day to day, it was easy work. I rarely had to deliver beat downs and had time enough to myself for a social life, but I'd not made any actual friends, and the women I knew only saw me on the clock. That usually proved to be enough because most of those girls were eager and chatty and kept believing they'd soon catch a break and be fashion models or real estate brokers or actresses or whatever. Anything but the sort of women who took money for sex from a guy like me.

Maybe some of them succeeded. I don't really know. There was one I stuck with after a while and gave up all the others because I'd decided (the way men will sometimes) that she'd come around one evening and not take money anymore. That never happened. Instead, after half a year, she raised her rates and stopped talking to me about her hopes and plans.

I saw her picture some months later in one of those slick beachside magazines. She'd married a man who was three or four times her age, and he appeared to have taken a chunk of his wealth and brought his bride a new set of lips. Breasts too, by the looks of her, and a slightly smaller chin. She came off looking odd and weary and a little desperate for youth. At the time, I doubt she was much over thirty-two.

I took walks after that, usually by myself, though I did occasionally go with the dog of the woman who lived just down the hall. Her hips were shot, and her dog was ancient but still hardy and active somehow even though he ate mostly Sara Lee pound cake and peanut butter from a spoon.

His name was Jubal. The woman told me why, but I couldn't really follow, and he had a frosty white snout and a foot he couldn't really put much weight on, but he got along well on the other three and was usually up for a couple of miles. I would have picked up after him like good citizens do but for the fact that he was almost always squirting. When he peed, he'd squat all cockeyed and pretty thoroughly hose himself.

Ok, so maybe not truly happy, but I was content for a long stretch down in Dade, and even once we'd moved across the state to work out of Tampa and spots north, I missed Jubal but still got along well enough. Uri made loans and investments. He sold odd lots of contraband for exorbitant considerations, and he got away with almost everything because of who and how he was. While the Czech in Pompano was worth avoiding because he was erratic, Uri with his snips had built a reputation of being reliable to a fault. You met your terms with him or soon enough you couldn't hold a fork.

Uri was the sort of pure thing people don't see much of in this world.

So we were fine, me and him, and would have stayed that way if I hadn't brought my little brother into the mix. He'd made a hash of something back home. I was never entirely clear on the details because by the time he called me he was already at Schiphol waiting on his Atlanta flight. He asked if I could put him up for a week or two because he felt sure his mess would soon enough blow over and he could go back home.

"Is somebody dead?" That's all I ever asked him.

He took a very long time saying, "No."

I was in Tallahassee when he landed, and he rode a bus as far as Albany where I picked him up. The only English Osip had was what he'd learned from television, and yet he'd convinced them at immigration he was coming to fetch his fiancée. He was carrying in his wallet an old snapshot of our cousin, a brawny girl with whiskers named Galina. In that picture, she was eating an onion raw and helping to haul a boat. I guess Osip got into the country out of an overabundance of pity.

He could stay for two weeks legally and told me that would be long enough. It wasn't, of course, because whatever he'd done, he'd done it to all the wrong people, the kind who store slights away for later and never, in fact, forget. Osip remained convinced his knotty mess would somehow become untangled because he hadn't yet learned that messes hardly ever do.

So I endured his optimistic chatter but knew better than to buy it, and I started angling on how to place him while he was still thinking he'd go home. I kept him out of sight for the best part of a month, or I'd leave him anyway at my place when I'd go off to work. I gave him firm instructions to stay close by and steer away from people, but he ran up a tab at the lounge down the street by claiming to work for Uri, and they had to suppose that Osip was maybe a little psychotic himself, so they kept track of what he ordered but were too fond of their fingers to make him pay.

I'm sure Osip thought that was all good fun, but that lounge was owned by a couple of guys who were related to crime by marriage. They weren't active lawbreakers but they got regular requests to hold goods and money in their place, stuff they'd certainly do time for if it ever got found out. So they didn't much like one of Uri's boys passing afternoons in their bar.

I didn't know about any of this, of course, until it was too late to matter. I was trying not to think too hard about Osip or press him on what he was up to because I was aware that about half of everything he'd tell me wouldn't be true. That was leftover from back when we were boys, and he had the gift for talking his way out of almost anything. That's just the sort of talent that works for a man right up until it doesn't.

Since I suspected I was stuck with him, I started talking up Osip for work. I didn't make anything like a hard pitch to Uri, but I mentioned my brother had shown up and was available for errands and dodgy bits of business if Uri had any come up.

"He like you?" Uri asked me and then made a fist and raised it my way.

I shook my head and told him back, "Slicker. Likes to talk."

"Drive too?"

I nodded, and that's how it started for Osip. He got sent to Pensacola in a flatbed rental truck to pick up a sofa and a bedroom suite Uri was taking as an installment from a long-time customer who'd found himself pinched for cash. Uri was letting the man buy two weeks of grace for the chance to pay later probably twice over what he owed. That was as close to a break as Uri would ever allow.

Osip took a guy named Jacko with him. He was half Cuban and half Creek Indian and ordinarily said about fourteen words a day. He could sit very still and tolerate people, wait hours for instructions, and then do in silence exactly what he'd been told.

I imagine Osip practiced his English on Jacko all the way up and around the coast and probably pumped Jacko for some Uri info which, knowing Jacko, was sparse and useless. Jacko cut Uri's grass and trimmed his bushes. He moved stuff around when that was required, but Jacko couldn't drive, and he was too upstanding to ever break the law. On top of that, he was mentally deficient, so Jacko wasn't equipped to have anything like piercing insight into Uri. He probably told Osip Uri was nice except sometimes when he wasn't.

They came back with not just the furniture but also a brand new motor scooter.

"Came with," Osip told me as he gestured toward the bed and the dresser and wardrobe.

"Oh yeah?" I put that to Jacko who shook his head and told me, "No."

So Osip tried to "remind" Jacko that yes, in fact, the man with the furniture had told them to take the scooter as well. Osip refreshed Jacko on where he'd said it and what they'd been up to at that moment, but Jacko was the type who knew what had happened and wouldn't be "reminded" into saying something else.

Osip saw what he was up against and shifted course right away. "Somebody left it beside the road," he said.

Jacko told me, "They didn't."

"Get it down," I told Osip and then took charge of that scooter once it was on the ground.

I rolled it over to a boggy patch and then on through to a swamp, which was just deep enough to hide the thing once I'd laid it over.

Osip complained all the while in Russian and English and a spot of Greek he'd picked up from an old girlfriend.

I let him tire out and fall silent before I told him the one thing he needed to know if he hoped to keep working for Uri. "Follow directions. Only do what he says."

Uri was particular about that sort of thing. He didn't tolerate freelancing or any variety of improvisational graft. You did what he wanted how he preferred or he'd pull his snips out on you.

"Some way somehow," I told Osip, "Uri always knows."

He did too. It was like he could smell the enterprising betrayal when his employees tried to capitalize on their proximity to him. It galled him because he was the psychotic self-starter with the ready talent for harm while the rest of us only got up to custodial trifles for a wage. At least I did Uri the service of being an available human buffer and driving the man around. Osip had only moved furniture. Uri didn't even know his name.

"See if you can be a little careful," I told my brother, "for a while."

I had to think that was the best I could hope for from him. Osip was bound for thievery or worse because he'd decided nothing would ever touch him since nothing ever had, including some guy talking Yiddish half the time who couldn't be bothered to wear socks, which was the built-in danger of Uri. If you didn't tune into his eyes, he looked like just another oldster wandering around the sunshine state.

ii

So I knew there'd be a reckoning, but I did all I could to put it off. I got my brother on regular with a branch of Uri's business that Uri didn't trouble himself with much. Osip collected from builders between Tampa and Fort Myers who'd signed on with Uri to get their lumber and siding and masonry cheap, most of it freightered in from China and spirited away at the docks.

That was one of Uri's early ventures before he'd struck the proper balance between labor and return. He let it keep going because it still sort of paid, but he had virtually no interest in it. So that was a perfect job for Osip who could chisel around the edges without drawing any notice. That was the plan anyway until Osip skimmed enough goods to build three houses in Bonita Springs. He went in with a contractor from Albania, and the two of them split the profits. Those houses even stood for nearly a year before a hurricane blew them flat when it became apparent that they'd been thrown together out of code.

It took one industrious county inspector to make all the trouble Osip needed. He was a decent, honest gentlemen who refused to be bought off. He wouldn't be warned off either. Osip brought me in for that. I followed him home and jostled him a little in his driveway.

I could see he was scared. He was just some wiry guy in a Member's Only jacket. I shoved him around and made the sort of threats you make, even suggested I might just bust up his wife after I'd done with her what I pleased. He only had to drop the Bonita Springs stuff and move onto something else. I even stuck some cash in his trouser pocket in a bid to help him along.

"Yes, sir," he told me. That was all he said. He never got more specific. It was just "Yes, sir" to every order I gave him and every suggestion I made.

Even then I could see he was hardly the sort of man you could purchase. He was just putting me off until he could work out how to be honest again. I doubted snipped fingers and toes would even have won him over entirely. He'd been hired to do a job for the county, and he'd do it no matter what.

So I knew it was just a matter of time before the trouble got back to Uri because his crew had boosted the building supplies and his trucks had moved them along. Eventually, he would be setting his sights on my brother and his Albanian colleague. That meant the only chance for Osip was if he bailed and moved along, and that wasn't even a sure thing since Uri could be dogged, but it's a big country, and finding Osip would take time. That left open the chance that Uri would get distracted by other business or, better still, meet his maker and leave all of us alone.

I gave Osip the benefit of my advice and described to him the way that Uri had handled another couple of guys who'd helped themselves to a slice off the top. They worked together moving hash, and Uri had supplied some of their funding, which they missed two payments on.

Those fellows didn't know Uri all that well, hadn't done their homework on him and weren't aware of how poorly he tolerated their brand of disrespect.

So they came willingly on a boat ride where they made to Uri a promise that they'd never ever be delinquent again. Uri allowed that was a promise those two boys were certain to keep, and then he had us bring out the cinder blocks and chains. Everything got a lot less jolly after that.

I told my brother the whole sorry tale, but he'd lost interest by the end. That sort of thing would never happen to him because it never had.

Osip refused to leave town, much less the state, and he stayed optimistic that he wouldn't get found out, which might have been how things would have gone but for that Albanian builder who broke under questioning from one of Uri's men. Then Uri shared with me that builder's account of what he'd gotten up to with my brother.

"So?" Uri asked me.

I told him I didn't know a thing about it, but I added I'd been acquainted with some Albanians previously and hadn't trusted a single one.

"We'll have a *shmuesn*, yes?"

I'd attended a couple of Uri's *shmuesns*. They usually started out cordial enough, but then Uri would get to the nut of the thing and rain down some form of violence.

What else could I do but nod and say, "*Shmuesn*. Yes. All right."

I bought my brother a day and a half by insisting I couldn't find him and then telling Uri I wouldn't be surprised if Osip had gone back home. Uri, though, said he would be surprised and showed me Osip's passport. That was just the brand of insurance Uri routinely liked to hold.

"*Shmuesn*?" he asked me another time.

I had no real choice after that. So I rounded up Osip and told him the big boss wanted a chat. He wasn't bothered much by the prospect, but not being bothered much was his way, and I drove him where Uri had told me to and put him out of the car. There was another guy there. Big Frank, they called him, and he grabbed Osip by the arm and walked him out of sight.

I went home and waited, though I can't say for what exactly since I'd been around Uri long enough to have a fair sense of how things would go. I wouldn't hear from Osip again. I wouldn't really hear much from Uri beyond some phlegmy Yiddish chestnut meant to explain this world away. And that's pretty much how it played out. Osip simply wasn't anywhere anymore, and the following morning Uri inflicted on me a spot of Yiddish chatter that had to do with a lamb who'd worked himself into a thicket, and every time he bucked and butted, he only made things worse.

Then Uri had me carry him to meet a client in a diner, and I circled the block on foot a few times to help let the pressure off. We never mentioned my brother between us again. He'd paid the price for his offense, and Uri considered the matter closed and balance restored. He was big on equilibrium. That's how he thought of it anyway, but it was all about Uri visiting harm until he felt unoffended.

I'd long made like I had let it go, like I too subscribed to balance and would take balance over and above any itch for compassion in this life. But I didn't know how to let it go, so I shoved it down and kept it hidden and would regularly wake up in the night with my brother on my mind.

So I was already heading nowhere good when we hit the road for Virginia, and I'd spy spots along the way and catalog them in my head, places where I had to think Uri's carcass might go undiscovered. At the top of my list was a particularly inviting mass of sticker bushes behind a half-collapsed AME church about midway through South Carolina. Most nights when I thought of my brother, I pictured those sticker bushes as well.

I didn't have a plan, though, just regular jolts of animosity. I realized after a while I was doing what Osip had been doing all along, just waiting to bump into an active chance.

I didn't even know I'd finally met one when that man came out of the house. It was hard to tell what he was up to because he wasn't right and normal. His chatter sounded even worse than Yiddish, and he had a limp and a stagger and a twitch or two as well like he never knew, when he set off, where exactly he'd end up.

I wasn't altogether convinced those people had much to do with anything. It was strange to come all that way just to find a cop I remembered a little because, like Uri, he'd had run-ins with Osip too. He appeared to have an interest in the girl we'd come across. Uri only wanted his gemstones, that and the chance to lop a couple of Viktor's digits. Those two ladies on the front walk were up to their own thing, and one of them had a haircut like you'd see in a cartoon. Add to all that the man on the asphalt who'd been kicked and stomped but still just kept on talking, kept on spelling something at us.

I knew Uri had made his mind up not to leave without his gemstones, even if he didn't seem to believe they'd end up being worth awfully much. Those gems had moved from liquid asset into principle for Uri, which meant he'd search until he found them, and then somebody would get hurt. Almost certainly Viktor who I'd be charged with holding down.

So I could see life unspooling before me, could picture what I'd be up to over the course of the next day or so, and that was the sort of stuff in my head when the man with the pistol came toward us. He was holding it in a funny way as he crossed the yard in our direction. Not by the handle but up near the barrel, and he sure couldn't shoot it from there.

The woman with the regular hair called out to stop him, but he didn't pay her any attention and just kept heading in Uri's direction. That's what it looked like to me anyway. He appeared to be going for Uri and the girl.

He was moving fairly slowly, looked to be fighting to keep his balance, and once he got within six feet of Uri and little baby-cakes, he stopped walking and started fooling with his gun.

By then, I could see it was in pieces, and he was trying to hold it together. The barrel and the handle and cylinder were not remotely in line. So he fiddled and he fussed and was slow enough about it to give Uri the chance to decide he didn't want to get shot by a cripple. So Uri pulled out his snips and raised them high. He could use them like a dagger when he wanted. And here he came across to set the man straight in what promised to be a homicidal way.

I only needed about a half step to catch Uri with my shoulder. He cut loose with a spot of satisfying racket as he lifted off the ground and then dropped to the pavement without getting so much as a hand out to break his fall.

His breath left when he landed, and he told all of us, "Grrhmmfft." Not Yiddish as far as I could tell, but then not English either.

ELETRIPTAN

The truth is I'm off my meds because they got a little pricey, especially once I got hit with a bill for Leon I hadn't counted on. You wouldn't think it would cost much of anything to keep a squirrel at home, but Leon's overbite got infected, and the fever ran clean through him, so it was pay up or shove him into a shoebox and stick him in the ground. The vet left us alone to weigh our options, and Leon did that thing with his tiny front feet where he barely sinks his little claws into my finger.

If I'm honest, I've got Leon now instead of almost anything else.

I nearly had a wife once and probably would have married the girl if she'd been more pushy and had insisted I choose between the guys and her. I have to suspect she got a whiff that I was deeply conflicted. I could perform well enough if she gave me ample warning, but she might have noticed it all appeared to be easier for me with the boys.

I like to think of it as Roman, a kind of gladiator thing. Us guys have been tumbling around together for a considerable while, and we don't have to worry about being rough and hurting each other's feelings. Mostly it's beer and a few hands of poker, but I'll admit there were more than a couple of times when I went in for something else. There were six or eight months there when I hung out with a fellow named Matt from out in the valley. He had a Harley. I had one too, and that was enough for a while, but after we'd gotten tight and had done all the ordinary stuff men do, we had a night in a motor lodge, and then another and another.

We never talked about it. It was just one of those things that happened and kept happening until Matt's wife caught on and managed to reel him back in. It was hard to find another Matt. I like to think I had near misses. I also ended up on a roadhouse floor with one of my molars down my throat, and that proved enough to put me off of the Roman way from there on out. By then, I was too fat and tattooed to hold much charm for present- able women, so instead of a foot in both worlds, I wasn't stand- ing in either one.

I had a decent job helping to steer delinquents out of delin- quency, had a house I nearly owned outright, a cable package, and a Honda. I'd held onto my bike but didn't ride it anymore, kept it under a bedsheet in the carport, and ever since the road- house beating, I suffered from headaches I could barely abide. I wasn't fit for company and was feeling pitiful about it when I found tiny, helpless Leon laying in the yard.

He'd come out of a nest. His eyes were still closed, and he squeaked and squealed and wiggled around when I picked him up. A year or so before, I probably would have tossed him in the ditch and let the raccoons or the foxes or the chickenhawks have at him, but he needed me just when I needed him, so I carried him into the house.

I'd known a Leon back when I was a boy who'd had teeth like a squirrel, so the name popped into my head, and I decided to stick with it. I would have thought a little harder and gone with something more exotic, but I felt fairly certain Leon wouldn't make it through the night, most especially since the only milk I had was hazelnut coffee creamer. I'd dip a paper towel in it and let him suck on that.

I fooled with him for a couple of hours and then put him in a sock that I laid in my coffee table drawer. I went to bed and got up in the morning expecting to find him dead and throw him out, but he was still squeaking and screeching and grabbing my finger with his tiny claws, so I went to the store to buy proper milk and a box of plastic drink straws that I'd fill and then let

Leon suck them dry.

He opened his eyes maybe two days later and was soon enough living on peanut butter and sacks of sunflower seeds. I bought a birdcage at the Goodwill and fixed it up for Leon with an old bath towel and a bowl for water, a foil tart tin for nuts. But once he'd polished off the nuts, he ate the tin as well and then had a go at the wooden perch and the wire hinges on the cage door.

I figured I ought to put Leon outside once he seemed able to climb a tree. I didn't, however, but gave him the run of the house instead, and he all but disappeared for about three weeks. I'd hear him sometimes and occasionally glimpse him climbing the draperies or racing across a wall. He also ate through the Cheerios box on the kitchen counter and drank out of the dishes I'd leave to soak in the sink.

So I had a pet squirrel for a little while the way people usually have roaches or mice. I cornered him one night when I got up to pee and found Leon in the bathtub. He stayed long enough for me to say I required him to settle down because I wasn't about to live with a squirrel running free just as he pleased. I've had dogs before and a couple of cats, and I always explain things to them, give them a full accounting of what exactly I won't stand for and why. Sometimes they listen. Mostly they don't, but it strikes me as fairer than swatting them with a broom.

So I had a chat with Leon for as long as he'd permit it, and I chose to think him enough of a decent sort to take some of it in. That talk might be why he showed up on my nightstand two nights later and made himself a nest of sorts in my Kleenex box. From then on, that's where I'd find him after I'd put out most of the lights, so I left his cage open, stuck his food in there, and he'd just come and go.

I'd take him to work sometimes and show him off to the crew I was counseling. They were kids mostly, usually eighteen or nineteen, who'd gotten arrested and were doing county time. They usually came from crap families or bad romances. The guys often had kids already but didn't know how to take care of anything, so I'd hand one of them Leon to let them see what nurturing might be like.

Leon would climb up their pants legs sometimes or slip under their shirts and make them squirm. Even the ones who were disgusted at first and thought he was merely vermin would almost always warm to Leon once they'd held him long enough.

A girl came through the program. Evie. She was dark and plump and Polish and had a baby that lived with her mother and a dog that had ended up at the pound. She was in for petty larceny, more counts than she could skate on, and I could tell that minding Leon made her think.

"I ought to be better about all this stuff."

She had Leon on her shoulder, and it was just me and her in there talking while I tidied and packed up.

"I didn't want a pet squirrel," I informed Evie, "but there he was just out in the yard. Life's like that sometimes. You're off to get the mail and instead you end up with Leon."

I remember feeling emotional about Leon just then. The kids I talk to don't ordinarily react much to what I say, but that doesn't mean I can't find stuff I tell them moving on my own. Evie was softer than the rest of them though, seemed to stay on the edge of weepy because getting arrested (I guess) and locked up in county had knocked some starch out of her.

"This life," I told her, "will give you things to love, so what do you need to do?"

"Love them, I guess," is what she said, and then she laid a hand to my arm, the one with the iron cross, the scorpion, the skull, and the double strand of barbed wire, and told me moistly, "I miss my baby, C-Bog." It didn't sound like she meant the dog.

I was touched in that moment and went a little moist myself as I reached across and lifted Leon off of Evie's shoulder. I felt like I'd helped to open her up in a genuine way, partly because she'd called me C-Bog, which none of the rest of them ever would, but mostly because she'd gone (if only briefly) from being an inmate to a mother.

So I felt like I'd made a useful move and done a helpful thing until she told me a little more about her "baby". His name was Derrick. He drove an IROC and had muscles all over the place.

So I shifted to drawing my consolation exclusively from her C-Bog and reminded myself that reaching troubled youth was hardly a science. I let Leon ride in the glove box all the way home.

At first, I half believed that Leon was helping with my headaches. I'd been plagued with them ever since I woke up on that roadhouse floor, and Leon gave me something to think about other than my pain and problems. That was enough for a while, but then I guess I got used to having a squirrel around and so relaxed into letting those headaches circle back.

I lived with them for a while and made do with aspirin, but they gave me stomach trouble and didn't do much for the pain, so I popped into one of the drive-by clinics and got referred by them to a doc who had me scanned and tested and then gave me all sorts of brochures about living with migraines, but he was also good for some pills that, to hear it from him, he didn't want me to take.

"There's the potential for addiction," is how he put it.

I made noises about being careful, but I remember wondering if that didn't apply to most things in this life.

I told him I'd be careful but then brought home the pills and got hooked on Eletriptan anyway. The stuff didn't make me feel one way or another. I guess maybe it helped with my headaches, but I think I got fixated mostly because a doctor had warned me I might.

Otherwise, I had a job where I accomplished awfully little and ended up twice a week with a roomful of inmates because their keepers had made them show up. Beyond that, I had a pet squirrel I'd tried a few times to return to the wild because he was gnawing all my furniture and leaving messes in the house, but he'd just come back to the kitchen window whenever I put him out and cling to the screen making squirrelly racket until I'd let him back in.

I didn't have any actual friends anymore, just neighbors I'd see every now and again and occasionally quarrel with. I found one of my old girlfriends online and tried to get back up with her. She eventually sent me a Christmas photo of her entire family. Her husband was wearing a Santa hat. Her two girls had on floppy antlers, and my former girlfriend was dressed as a sexy elf in some kind of green tunic and heels.

So I failed to branch out but just stayed like I was, kept doing what I'd been doing with the addition of barking at neighbors when I decided they'd gotten too loud. I still had headaches, but my prime motivation for storming out of my house was interacting with regular humans because I spent most of my time with a squirrel and more than a little with honest-to-God delinquents. So I was hungry for truck with regular people in an ordinary sort of way, but since I wasn't quite built for ordinary, I'd go outside and yell.

I did finally meet all of my neighbors after twelve years on the block, but I'm sure none of them liked to see me coming because I was always pissy, full of threats and indignation and pharmaceutical prickishness. I was Clarence Bogarde, neighbor in a fury, and if even one of them had called me C-Bog the way I'd asked them to, I might have cooled down a couple of notches only been ill-humored. But since they all stuck with Clarence, I stayed migrained up, and I'd hear a blower or a loud voice and out the door I'd go.

For a while there, I had an ongoing spat with Russell across the street because he was a bad one for tooting his horn whenever he came or went. It got to where I'd hear him start his car and tighten up all over. He'd often blow it twice to let, I guess, his wife know he was leaving, but the chances seemed better than average she was aware of that already since he'd put on his uniform and left the house.

In the evenings, he'd come home and do it again, even worse

and more most days. So I jawed with Russell quite a lot. I'd go out and give him chapter and verse on the state of my condition.

"Right, yeah, elipan," he'd usually say or something a lot like it.

Russell was why I started spelling because he couldn't get anything straight. Then he'd give me a wink and a click as he shot me with his finger pistol. Russell would go in his house and leave me out there feeling unsatisfied.

His wife was more of a gamer. She's got kind of a sharp tongue and wasn't above going after me for being fat and tatted, particularly those times when I'd come on a little too strong.

She'd hear me out about my migraines and say something like, "Probably a tumor." Then she'd sometimes pick out a tattoo and pretend it was a thing it wasn't. "Nice goat," she told me one time about the jaguar on my calf.

I knew she was trying to get at me, but that hardly kept me from getting got. Dottie was also a bad one for calling me Clarence in a provocative way. She'd do it over and over because she knew how badly I wanted C-Bog. That was her way of telling me, "Dream on, princess." She could tell it stirred me up.

If I'm honest, I got to where I'd look forward to jousting with the woman. I found I had to admire the way she could slice me up, and I came to believe she had to care a bit to ridicule me, that she couldn't dismantle me out in the street and not give a hoot as well.

I tried being pleasant a time or two. I'd go outside when I saw her coming or going, and I'd have worked up something to say in the way of ordinary chat. She'd usually glance at me like I'd broken wind and not even slow down at all.

So in time she just got outrage and migraine-related fury because I liked the way it felt to get belittled and scorched by Dottie. I think I fell a little in love with the woman while quarreling with her out in the road. It didn't matter to me that she wasn't much to look at. I knew I wasn't much to look at either. We were both of us chunky and wrinkled, and she wore house dresses shaped like sacks until Russell had his episode and she took over for him. Then she switched to a baggy uniform that came off like a sack with legs.

I felt for her because when Russell had his stroke, he left the hospital thoroughly infirm and in a rage about it. I'd hear him yelling from over inside their house. I call it yelling, but it was usually the brand of racket an indignant cow might make.

So I was even more sympathetic to Dottie than I'd been before. She'd work all day and then bring home baby food and special cans of protein drink for Russell who'd usually pitch some kind of fit as soon as she'd set foot in the house. Some days she'd load him up in the car and carry him to doctors (I guess), and he'd buck and struggle against her all the way out to their Ford.

I offered to help her once when I saw her having an especially hard time with Russell, but he raised such a fuss that she waved me off. It seemed clear Dottie had so awful much on her plate, that I made a point for a while of only bickering with my other neighbors, particularly a widow lady two doors down whose son lived with her and played the drums. He did it a little too often with his windows open, so I had plenty of opportunities to yell at them instead.

But then Russell came onto his porch one night and got into a bellowing match with a stranger, a tall and hairy and with a crease in his head like somebody had smacked him hard with a plank.

I stalked straight over and asked them both, "What's all this yelling about?"

Russell told me something I couldn't make out, and the big, hairy guy just ignored me.

"There's some things I want," he said to Russell. "I'll go in and get them, I guess."

Russell yelled. He'd shifted around to cut loose in the direction of the house, and that's along about when I reminded him that I was prone to migraines, which a doctor had prescribed me actual medicine for. I spelled the name of it three times straight.

"Hold on," big, hairy guy told me, so I spelled at him as well.

And it was only once Dottie came out and Russell turned in her direction that I noticed he was holding in his good hand what looked suspiciously like a gun. He was gripping it in the middle as if he had no idea how guns worked, but it was clearly some kind of revolver, the sort a cowboy might carry. I had to wonder right away who exactly Russell was hoping to shoot.

I would have asked Dottie to clear things up. It seemed like a fruitful topic, but before I could say a thing to her, Russell swung back around my way, and he all but jabbed me with the barrel of his pistol. That seemed reckless to me. I wouldn't have shoved him otherwise. Then the big, hairy guy picked me up off the ground and tossed me into the road because (I decided) he'd found me shoving Russell provoking.

I knew I'd be bringing the law into it before I hit the pavement. I had a friend on the force, a boy anyway I'd passed a couple of nights with when he was supposed to be off fishing. He didn't even require an actual threat to pick up his badge and head our way because there's little that men like him won't do to keep the lie they've got.

The funny thing was, I caught myself wondering if I'd ever been kicked before. That would be aside from back when I was a boy and a girl I liked kicked me in the stomach. Hard too. She was wearing a pair of new boots and had taken them as fit reason to go around kicking all sorts of things. She kicked her dog. She kicked her trash can. She kicked a stump in her yard but immediately yelped and wished she hadn't. That struck me as funny, so after I'd laughed, she came over and kicked me too.

Lying there in the street, I couldn't remember having been booted since, even though I'd been punched more than a couple of times. It hardly seemed right or justified, but whenever I'd raise an objection, one of them would lay into me again.

I'd have thought the big one with the chewed-up ear would been the hardest on me, but it was the one in the chinos and loafers who really knew how to kick. He had smooth action and good rhythm, built up appreciable force. He impressed me as one of those guys devoted to doing things just so.

He'd managed to bust a couple of ribs. I was aware of that acutely, and it was in my power not to tempt him to crack a couple of more. I just had to stay where I was and groan, but I couldn't help myself and chimed in about my headaches and the medicine I'd been taking.

I even got about halfway through it before he laid into me again. This time loafer man went comprehensive. He even turned loose of his girl so he could draw both arms back and gain a bit of leverage. I lost count somewhere in the middle, but I think he kicked me a dozen times. As I caught a couple in the head, I heard somebody suggest he simmer down.

I thought maybe it was the one with the ear, but it was the other guy by the Chevy. He was puffy and sweaty, had a scab on his nose, and he called loafer man by his name.

"Let it go, Uri," is what he said.

I felt sure I'd never met a Uri, and this one didn't seem foreign at all until he said a thing to Chevy guy that wasn't exactly English.

It started out *Az Got zol voynen,* or something like it and went on from there. He kept giving me the loafer as he offered a translation. "If God lived on earth," he told us all, "people would break his windows."

I felt like that should mean something significant to me, given my situation. The man by the Chevy didn't seem to be deciphering any better than I was.

"Yeah, whatever," he said.

Uri kept on busting me up even though I hadn't spelled Eletriptan at him in a while.

Then fortunately for me, the man got distracted by a car coming down the road, an old brown car that stopped just barely short of where we were.

Somebody inside it said, "Told you."

Doors opened, and people got out.

Uri said something else that wasn't remotely English before he told us all, "Let a pig in the house, and it'll crawl on the table."

I couldn't help but believe, even down on the pavement, this Uri was a singular sort of guy.

I had to shift a little to see who'd come, and at first, I could only make out some filthy boy who wasn't wearing a shirt. Not properly anyway. He had it sort of around his neck, and a bloody bandaid laid across one his nipples.

"Watch out," the boy said. "Got his scissors."

That's when I saw that Uri had something in his hand.

"He's who you want," the girl dressed like a babydoll told him, and she pointed at the guy who'd put me on the pavement once before. I knew him immediately on account of the dent in his head.

"He's mine. I want a piece of him." That turned out to have come from the Greek looking boy in the trunk of the Chevy. The lid was open, and he was sitting up, but nobody appeared to be paying him much mind.

They were some kind of clippers in Uri's hand. I could tell that once I got a decent look. That seemed an odd thing for a man in chinos and loafers to carry around. Once he'd flipped the keeper off, the blades sprang open with a twang, and then Uri kicked me one time more to let me know I wasn't forgotten.

For the moment, Uri turned his attention to the big, hairy guy with the dent and waved those clippers at him just as Russell came out of the house. He half stumbled down the stairs and lurched across the yard. I heard Dottie tell him, "Stop!" and "Don't!" from over on the sidewalk, but Russell kept on coming, and I saw that he was carrying a thing as well.

I'd seen it before, and he was holding it wrong again. "Lord," I said, "he's got his gun."

Even I knew this was hardly the crowd to bring that weapon into, and Dottie and haircut must have known it as well because all of us together were telling Russell variations on "Don't" and "Stop."

He appeared to have a plan though, had clearly made up his mind about something and just kept coming until he was out in the street across from chino guy.

Russell told the man a thing at considerable length, but none of it came out sounding much like English. I couldn't make any sense of it. Uri, apparently, couldn't either until the big, hairy man with the dent in his head said, "He thinks you ought to leave."

Uri launched into a snatch of talk that wasn't English either, but before he could translate it for us, big, hairy weighed in again.

"He doesn't want you here anymore. Roughing up that woman. Kicking his friend. He says you'd best go on."

Even in my agony, I couldn't help but thrill a little at "friend." I'd been thinking I'd burned too many bridges for that.

"You tell him," Uri said, "nobody points a gun at me."

"You just told him," big, hairy guy said back. "Not a thing wrong with his ears."

The boy with the band aid had backed way up, and the Greek looking guy in the trunk of the Chevy had hunkered down and out of sight. Even the puffy man at the fender had retired maybe eight or ten yards.

It seemed clear that something awful was just about to happen, and chino man was exactly the sort of guy to help it along. True to form, he raised his clippers like he meant to do some stabbing, and then he walked in Russell's direction at double speed.

He couldn't have known from just looking that Russell's gun wouldn't shoot, that the thing was in three pieces, so I have to credit him for being bold where it came to that.

He probably would have cut Russell up. He was moving like he meant to when the man with the ear who'd driven him over shifted around to intervene. He took one step, which was all he needed to put a shoulder into Uri who went flying and then bounced on the asphalt. I could feel it when he hit.

The man with the ear relieved Russell of his gun, and it fell apart as he took it. Four pieces instead of three because Russell had found a bullet somewhere, and it rolled across the road.

I kept waiting for Chino to get up, but he hardly even moved, and everybody else appeared to take it easy for a moment. It was like the teacher had left the room. They all relaxed and started chatting. The puffy guy by the Chevy got into a conversation with the babycakes girl, and they were joined almost immediately by Dottie's friend with the haircut, while the man with the dent went over to have a back and forth with Russell.

Then together those two had a few words with the Greek looking boy in the trunk. It started as words anyway but then evolved into a quarrel and transitioned to a throttling when the big guy with the dent snatched up the guy and moved him rapidly from place to place.

He did it with quite a lot of vigor and kept causing that boy to bounce, which seemed to serve to both end their quarrel and snuff out their conversation.

It was shortly thereafter that the shirtless guy with the band aid on his nipple said, "Hey, y'all, look. He's bleeding all over the place."

The one with the ear turned Uri over. He must have landed on his snips and cut a vein somewhere because blood was leaving Uri at a pretty extravagant rate.

The lady with the haircut is the only one who spoke, and all she said was, "Hmm."

The guy with the ear put him back just like he'd been.

So there was enough going on to distract from how short my breath had become. It would turn out that one of my broken ribs had poked straight through a lung while the other one had jabbed my liver a little. I'd need four days in the hospital before I'd be fit to go home, and there'd be nothing to do but lie dead still and listen to my roommate gurgle. He had his head all wrapped up and didn't know who he was. A nurse or somebody had written his name in marker on his arm just in case he happened to wake up and see it. Norman.

There on the street, I was still thinking I'd get some tape around my middle, a couple of aspirin maybe, and then they'd send me home. I knew the drill. I'd busted ribs before. But then I tried to sit up and found out this was different.

That's when Dottie came over. She'd seen I was struggling. She stooped down and managed to join me on the pavement after a while. She'd gotten big, and we'd gotten old, so she couldn't just squat but had to lower herself while she held onto stuff. Various parts of that Chevy at first along with Russell's pant leg.

She sized me up and laid a hand lightly on my shoulder.

"Oh, C-Bog," is what Dottie said.

MAZEL TOV

Yeah. So. *Oy.* It's hard to tell if I'm cold or hot.

The guy from Panama City in orthopedic shoes with his toes all shrunk and knobby like they should have been on a monkey. He gave me such a look when I brought out the snips, thought being deformed would make him immune.

That neighbor girl from home with the white spot on her tooth. I might have been ten, but I'd already killed a dog and crippled a cat. She couldn't have known it but steered clear of me anyway. I told her I loved her, tried it out on her twice. The first time she laughed. The second time I pushed her into a ditch. Her father came around and picked me up by my hair.

I can hear them all talking. One of them even turns me for a look but then puts me straight back down just like I was. I feel like I know him a little but can't quite say from where.

They hate it when you drop them in the water because they've made their peace with losing just a big toe or a thumb. Then you bring out the chains and the cinder blocks, and that turns the corner for them. The fat one from Rego Park who'd relocated to Miami couldn't stop crying and wouldn't hold still, begged us just to shoot him instead. I remember thinking there'd be no lesson in that.

Gleb. That's him. Boils on his neck and an ear in about four pieces. I'd have changed that to Dave or something. He was probably raised on cabbage and parts of a cow nobody should eat. Got right in my way. Like running into a sofa. Smells around here of metal and asphalt both.

Yeah. So. *Oy.* I remember the boy, the kind used to getting away with everything. He couldn't believe it was over for him even when he was sinking down. They say the fish eat you, pick you clean, and the salt water and the barnacles turn the rest to powder.

Maybe losing your little brother's like getting picked up by your hair. You simmer about it and fix it later. I found her daddy after a while.

Shtek nit dem kop tsum volf in moyl arayn. Don't stick your head in the mouth of the wolf.

People would have been around by now if people were coming to help me. I'd like to shiver but can't manage it. Osip, that's what it was. Stings a little here at the last. Let's see where I end up.